3

Please turn to the back of the book for
an interview with Graham Thomas.

MALICE
IN
LONDON

By Graham Thomas
Published by The Ballantine Publishing Group:

MALICE IN THE HIGHLANDS
MALICE IN CORNWALL
MALICE ON THE MOORS
MALICE IN LONDON

MALICE IN LONDON

Graham Thomas

FAWCETT BOOKS • NEW YORK

A Fawcett Book
Published by The Ballantine Publishing Group
Copyright © 2000 by Gordon Kosakoski

All rights reserved under International and Pan-American Copyright Conventions. Published in the United States by The Ballantine Publishing Group, a division of Random House, Inc., New York, and simultaneously in Canada by Random House of Canada Limited, Toronto.

Fawcett Books and colophon are trademarks of Random House, Inc.

www.randomhouse.com/BB/

ISBN 0-7394-1068-7

Manufactured in the United States of America

For Aunt Hedi

From the cities of nine
Days' night whose towers will catch
In the religious wind
Like stalks of tall, dry straw
           —DYLAN THOMAS
Author's Prologue, *Collected Poems 1934–1952*

MALICE IN LONDON

PROLOGUE

The river looked like tar, sludging along, full of filth, she fancied as she hurried along the quay. She was searching for her dog, Hamish, a terrier of indeterminate lineage who had a predilection for the well-bred cats that infested the Bermondsey docks these days. It was a raw night in March and the damp in the air was palpable, a thick congealing mist that seeped through the fabric of her raincoat into her aching joints. She paused to catch her breath, gathering her collar tightly around her in a vain attempt to keep out the chill.

She glanced nervously about. There was not another soul in sight. Behind her loomed the gothic silhouette of Tower Bridge, its presence more felt than seen in the fog. Up ahead she could see the reassuring glow of the row of shops and restaurants below a block of converted warehouse flats. She scolded herself for being so nervy. Nowadays you were unlikely to encounter anybody more sinister than a stockbroker on the docks and, besides, who would be interested in bothering an old woman? Still, she thought, she had better collect her dog and get home before she caught her death.

"Haaamish!" she called out in a quavering voice. There was no response, so she continued on her way, her footsteps sounding hollowly on the pavement. She picked up her pace slightly as she passed a dark, boarded-off construction site. Eventually, she found herself in front of a derelict warehouse, one of the few remaining vestiges of the Thames's commercial past that had not yet succumbed to the property developers. Just ahead was St. Saviour's Dock, a narrow tidal inlet off the river. The channel was crossed by a footbridge and was lined on the far side by smart flats with pink and blue balconies. She shivered convulsively. At that moment she wanted nothing more than to cross over the footbridge and nip back home to put the kettle on.

She looked up at the dripping brickwork of the old Butler's Wharf warehouse with its rusted iron doors and stairways and gaping black windows. Her Harry had worked on these docks after the war in the heyday when London was still the largest port in the world and thousands of ships of all types and sizes crowded the six-mile stretch of river downstream from the Tower, carrying exotic cargoes from the far-flung outposts of the Empire. There were times, particularly after a fresh rain, when she could smell the faint perfume of cinnamon and cloves that still permeated the timbers of the old buildings. She gave an involuntary sigh. Everything had changed in the Sixties when the container ships all moved to Tilbury and Harry went on the dole. Mustn't wallow in it, she told herself, but it was hard to accept the gentrification of her old neighborhood.

"Where is that naughty dog?" she said aloud, getting truly cross now. She'd give him a proper scolding when he came back. Maybe he'd chased a cat into the old warehouse—

Her train of thought was interrupted by a faint whimpering sound. "Hamish?" she called out doubtfully. She strained to listen, but all she could hear was the river lapping against the pilings and the sound of her own breathing. She frowned. Perhaps it had been a rat.

Without knowing why exactly, she walked over to the concrete parapet and peered over. An iron ladder descended to the river; the pitted wall was stained with streaks of rust. She stared into the black, oily water and shuddered. The Thames had supposedly been cleaned up to the point where even a few foolhardy fish had ventured back, but she reckoned it would still kill you if you fell in. She was about to turn away when she suddenly froze.

There was a commotion at the base of the ladder. She stared, uncomprehending, as a hand rose slowly from the water and grasped the bottom rung. Then a head appeared and another arm, fingers splayed, stretching toward her. She could see the face now, festooned with strands of hair like seaweed, its mouth contorted into a silent scream. Before she could react, the body slipped back and disappeared beneath the surface of the water like a half-remembered dream.

CHAPTER 1

From the window of his study, Powell surveyed the wasteland of his back garden and speculated once again about what Marion would say when she returned from Canada at the end of summer. The list of chores he should have done but didn't, and the things he could still do but probably wouldn't, encroached on his mental landscape like so many weeds. He had dutifully read Marion's voluminous instructions, a sort of horticultural *à la recherche du temps perdu*:

Apply manure and fertilizer, plant onion sets and shallots, warm up soil with cloches [cloches?], *start sowing vegetables without protection* [was this wise?], *sow early kitchen crops in cold frames, plant new strawberries, chit* [?] *seed potatoes, fertilize fruit bushes if needed* [how in heaven's name was he to judge this?], *plant gladioli bulbs, sow hardy annuals* [exactly which hardy annuals were not specified, so he felt that he could hardly be held accountable for not doing this], *feed and mulch beds and borders, take chrysanthemum cuttings, start off begonia tubers, and pot up chrysanthemum cuttings started earlier* [ha!].

And that was just the first page covering early spring.

Powell appreciated an attractive garden as much as the next person—he was simply content to leave the mechanics to those, like his wife, who had the aptitude for it. He had once read somewhere that in spring a true gardener thinks of birds and plump buds and cannot wait to start propagating. He could at least relate to that sentiment.

With his family away in Canada—Peter and David at university and Marion on sabbatical for a year—Powell found himself at loose ends. He supposed it was the lack of structure in his life, for want of a better word, that was the most difficult thing to adjust to. Not that his routine had changed appreciably—the daily commute by train to London and the drudgery of his job at the Yard. It was the weekends he missed most, when he could catch up with his sons' busy lives, tinker with his car, or just sequester himself in his study and read, with the domestic engine of the Powell household throbbing reassuringly all around him. Or perhaps do something with Marion, just the two of them, although there hadn't been much time for that in recent years. Increasingly, it seemed, they were leading more or less parallel lives, which converged only occasionally. And with Marion away pursuing her academic career, it appeared that they were presently on sharply divergent courses.

He glanced distractedly out the window again. The tulips looked all right, he supposed, trying to see the bright side of things. He could see the neighbor's Siamese cat creeping up on a robin beside the greenhouse. He wondered if they thought about him often. Who could blame them if they didn't? He knew better than anyone that he was hardly the model husband or father, but he sometimes wondered if he had it all to do over again, whether he would do anything differently. To avoid descending any further down that slippery slope, he turned his mind to another well-worn preoccupation: his nemesis, Sir Henry Merriman, Assistant Commissioner of the Metropolitan Police Service.

Sir Henry, thank God, had been unsuccessful in his recent bid for the top job, but he was now on the hunt for scapegoats, convinced that several of his senior officers, including Powell, had done him in. Powell was on decent terms with the new Commissioner, so he wasn't particularly worried. However, he'd have to watch himself—Merriman was utterly ruthless and, if nothing else, had shown a consummate talent for survival.

A movement in the corner of his eye caught his attention. The cat had pounced and pinned the robin to the lawn. He then lay down and proceeded to play with it.

Detective-Sergeant Bill Black affected a serious expression when Powell walked into the office the next morning.

"Gov'nor wants to see you, sir," he announced gruffly.

"O'Brien?"

Black nodded.

"What have I done this time?"

Black's wide face broke into a grin. "He wants some info on salmon fishing in Scotland."

The new Commissioner had recently taken up game fishing and had obviously heard that Powell had some experience in that line.

"The things I have to do to further my career."

"Put in a good word for me, would you, sir?"

Powell grimaced. "If you need a recommendation from me, you're really up the creek." He gulped down his coffee and headed over to the Commissioner's Suite.

A half hour later, as he was returning to his office, he bumped into Merriman.

"Where have you been, Powell," he snapped.

"Talking to Mr. O'Brien, sir," Powell replied innocently.

"What about?"

Powell glanced at the ceiling. "Personal matter, sir."

"You report to *me*, Powell. Don't ever forget that!" Merriman hissed.

"No, sir." Powell was beginning to enjoy himself. "Will that be all, sir?"

"No, that will not be all. I have a little job for you. I want you to look into the Brighton matter."

Richard Brighton, a former councillor on Southwark Council, had turned up dead in the Thames last month. How he got there wasn't entirely clear, but a random act of violence was the prevailing theory. Powell, guarded now, asked, "What exactly do you want me to look into?"

Merriman smiled smoothly, knowing that he had regained the advantage. "The local lads have taken the case about as far as they can, and it needs a clear-up, that's all. Given the profile of the case, it wouldn't be politic to leave any loose ends dangling."

Better to knot them around my bloody neck, Powell thought. By lumbering him with the Brighton case—the trail had already grown cold, by all accounts—Merriman was, in effect, squandering a precious Murder Squad assignment. Powell's name would now go the bottom of the list and it might be six months before he was called out again. The Area Major Investigations Pool (still colloquially referred to as the Murder Squad) was made up of senior detectives from the various Met Areas as well as New Scotland Yard. The Pool operated on the basis of a rotating list, with each team, consisting of a Chief Superintendent and a Detective-Sergeant, taking their turn. The AMIP was the only thing that kept him sane, the only opportunity amidst the bureaucratic inanity to do what he'd actually joined up for.

Merriman smirked. "Cat got your tongue, old man? I knew you'd be pleased; I know how much you enjoy getting out into the field."

Powell could barely contain his fury, but he said nothing.

"Good. You'd better get started then." Merriman turned on his heel and flounced off.

As Powell headed back to his office, he could not have known that both he and Merriman were dead wrong about the Brighton case.

That evening, Powell sat commiserating with Bill Black in the Fitzrovia Tavern in Charlotte Street.

The stocky sergeant raised his glass. "TGIF, eh, sir?"

"Cheers," Powell replied gloomily.

"Cheer up, Mr. Powell. There could be more to this one than meets the eye. I've had a look at the file, and there are one or two points of interest."

"Such as, Sherlock?"

Black leaned forward with an earnest expression. "Well, sir, you may recall that Brighton was involved in that controversy over the eviction of the council tenants in Rotherhithe. He must have made a few enemies along the way."

"Name a politician who hasn't." Powell eyed Black with interest. He had learned over the years that it was a mistake to ignore his assistant's instincts. Slow and methodical, some might even say plodding, Detective-Sergeant Black usually got there in the end.

Black persisted. "His wallet was missing, so the locals reckon it was a blagger who done it, but he could just as easily have lost it in the river."

"Idle speculation at this point," Powell observed antiseptically.

Black frowned. "You're right, sir. It just seems a bit extreme, that's all. To mug somebody is one thing, but coldblooded murder?"

Powell emptied his pint. "Your round, I think."

"Er, just a half for me, I think, sir. The missus will be expecting me. Fuller's, wasn't it, sir?"

Powell watched his assistant jostle for position at the bar. He lit a cigarette. The pub was doing a modest business that night. Just north of Oxford Street and Soho in the shadow of the British Telecom tower, it was a little off the beaten path for tourists and was frequented by an eclectic mix of students, broadcasting types, writers, and assorted poseurs, along with a few locals, mostly elderly, who actually lived in the neighborhood. Powell often came here for a pint or two after work, followed by a curry next door at the K2 Tandoori. The pub had a long literary history, having been a favorite haunt of writers and poets in the Forties. Poetry readings were still held in the dingy Writer's Bar downstairs. A poster in the window offered poetic entertainment on Thursday nights by the Cunning Linguist: AN EVENING OF ORAL PER-*VERSE*-ITY! Hardly Bohemia, but still more diverting, in Powell's estimation, than the majority of central London pubs.

"Getting back to the matter at hand," Powell said after Detective-Sergeant Black had resettled himself at their table, "I hope you're right about the Brighton case. I'd like nothing better than to rub Merriman's nose in something nasty."

"*I will feed fat the ancient grudge I bear him,* eh, sir?"

Powell smiled. Ever since Black had taken an evening class in English literature appreciation, he was forever spouting quotations, throwing down the literary gauntlet, as it were, to his superior. The unassuming sergeant was blessed with a near-photographic memory, which kept Powell on his toes. Taking his cue, Powell rose to the occasion. "Enough shop talk, Bill. *I prithee go and get me some repast.* Are you sure I can't interest you in a cheeky little *vindaloo* next door? Good for what ails you."

Opens up the sluices at both ends, you mean, Black mentally translated, based on hard experience living with his superior's culinary addiction. "Er, no, thank you, sir. The missus will have something on the go by now . . ." he trailed off awkwardly. He felt slightly guilty about abandoning his superior to his own devices, what with his family away in Canada and nothing but a lonely house to come home to each night. "Er, look, Mr. Powell, why don't you come along and have a bit of supper with us? Nothing special, but we'd love to have you. If it gets a bit late, we can make up the spare room for you. I'll call Muriel and—"

Powell smiled warmly. "Thanks, Bill, I appreciate the offer, but I wouldn't feel right imposing on your good lady on such short notice. Perhaps another time."

Black looked genuinely disappointed.

"Or I could have you both out to Surbiton some weekend. Do you know anything about gardening, by any chance?"

Black grinned. "Well, if you're sure, sir."

"Drink up. You don't want to be late."

"Right. Cheers." Black finished his beer with a prodigious swallow. "I'd best be off then. See you Monday."

After Black had gone, Powell sat for a few minutes lost in thought, blissfully unaware of the consequences of his failure to take up the Detective-Sergeant's offer of hospitality. Eventually, he stirred and wandered over to the bar to fetch another pint.

CHAPTER 2

Powell's favorite barmaid was in attendance that night, a young Canadian named Jill Burroughs, with whom he had struck up a professional relationship of sorts over the past few months: She dispensed the beer, and he drank it. She was pretty and personable and had a direct, guileless manner that Powell found refreshing. She had been working her way across Europe when she met a young man, a student at London University. She'd been living with him for about six months now. Powell and Jill had hit it off the moment they realized they had something in common, when she mentioned she was Canadian, and he'd told her about Marion and the boys. He supposed if he had a daughter, he would want her to be like Jill.

"I'll have another, please."

"Drowning our sorrows, are we, Chief Superintendent?"

"Just lubricating the little gray cells."

"I see." She slowly pulled the tap handle, filling a pint glass with foaming bitter. She placed it on the bar and looked at him. "Heard from the family recently?"

12

"Got a letter last week. I'll probably ring on the weekend."

"That's nice. That'll be one-sixty-five, please."

He fumbled for the coins. "Have your pound of flesh," he muttered jokingly.

He left the pub about nine-thirty and crossed Windmill Street to the K2 Tandoori. The proprietor, Rashid Jamal, was in a state of obvious agitation. The restaurant was packed, but Rashid seemed oblivious.

He accosted Powell at the door and whispered mysteriously, "I am needing your advice, my friend. I'll join you at your table in a moment."

Rashid returned a few minutes later with a large bottle of Cobra lager for Powell and an orange squash for himself. He sat down, his dark eyes blazing with a feverish intensity. "Have you seen this—this outrage?" He thrust over a crumpled clipping taken from one of the less uplifting Sunday tabloids. He sat fuming silently as Powell unfolded it and began to read.

It was a particularly scathing review of the K2 by a pompous and universally despised restaurant critic named Clive Morton:

Whilst slumming in Charlotte Street last week, I made the mistake of stopping in at the K2 Tandoori for dinner. In retrospect, the sign in the window should have warned me off: "Open seven days a week except Sunday." Not only is the proprietor, one R. Jamal, apparently unable to compose a coherent sentence in English, neither, it seems, can he read his Curry Club recipe book. The tandoori chicken was done like an old Wellington, the mint chutney was insipid and watery, and the okra had the slimy demeanor of the tinned species. Furthermore, I have little doubt that my companion's "lamb" started out life in an alley off Gerrard Street. Definitely one to avoid unless you have just come from a rugby match, having consumed ten or twelve pints, and only then because you will at least have the assurance that you and your meal will soon part company.

Powell handed the clipping back without a word.

"Slander, lies, untruths—it is an unspeakable abomination!" Rashid erupted. "If he ever comes here again, I will slice off his tiny bits and roast them in the tandoor. Ha! Let him review that!"

Several of the neighboring tables erupted in spontaneous applause.

Rashid bowed his head in a dramatic gesture of acknowledgment.

Powell smiled. "You see. Nobody really pays any attention to Clive Morton—the only reason they keep him on is to sell newspapers. I hear he's persona non grata in most of the decent restaurants in town."

Rashid appeared unconvinced. "Nonetheless, my friend, I am deeply wounded. I have devoted myself to my art, my restaurant. It is for me a point of honor. It is . . . my life."

Rashid was something of a prima donna in his own right and was arguably as opinionated as the restaurant critic, which only made things worse. Powell decided that a tangential approach would be best under the circumstances. He looked at his friend. "You can't imagine how much I look forward to these evenings, when I can forget my cares for a few hours, get together with an old friend, and indulge myself in the best Indian food in all of London."

His words had the desired effect. Rashid's eyes glistened and he was unable to speak for a few seconds. "Thank you, Erskine," he said eventually in a solemn voice. "I had forgotten for a moment my loyal customers. And my dear friends." He got to his feet with a flourish, once again the charming host. "Now, then. I shall bring you some *pappadams* while you consider the menu." He clapped his hands. "Ali! Another Cobra for Mr. Powell."

It was nearly eleven-thirty when Powell, fully replete, emerged from the K2 faced with the rather complicated problem of how to get home. The pubs were out, and there were still a few people in the street. He stared at his watch, trying to think coherently. The last train for Surbiton left Waterloo Station at 23:47. Or was it 23:54? He considered his options: try to find a cab or take the tube. He decided that the walk to Goodge Street Station would do him good. He should just be able to make—

"All dressed up and no place to go?"

It was Jill Burroughs just off work.

"On my way home, Jill. How 'bout you?"

"Same." She eyed him suspiciously. "What time does your train leave?"

"Oh, I've got about twenty minutes," Powell replied

cheerily, or as near to it as he could manage under the circumstances.

"You'll never make it!"

Powell considered this possibility for a moment. "I'll take a hotel room then."

"Nonsense. Come home with me. Stephen is away for the weekend. I can put you up on the sofa. You can catch a train first thing in the morning."

Powell recalled vaguely that Jill and her boyfriend shared a flat somewhere in Bloomsbury. He hesitated. He felt a bit silly.

Jill smiled. "I don't bite, Chief Superintendent."

Powell laughed. "All right, thanks." He took her arm. "Lead the way, Miss Burroughs. And, by the way, you can call me Powell."

The next morning, Powell awoke in Jill Burroughs's Bloomsbury flat with a head several sizes too large. Morning sunlight filtered through lacy curtains and the aroma of bacon and coffee stirred his senses. It took him a few moments to get his bearings. He was lying on a lumpy sofa under a duvet. He could see his clothes heaped on a chair across the room. He reached under the duvet and felt his shorts. Thank heavens for small mercies, he thought. He had little recollection of how exactly he'd got where he now found himself. He vaguely recalled walking down Windmill Street with Jill singing "Mellow Yellow," but that was about it. He winced at a sudden clanging of kitchen utensils.

A moment later, Jill popped her head into the sitting

room. "Back in the land of the living, are we?" she chirped.

Powell groaned.

"Up you get—you can't lie in bed all day. Breakfast will be ready in a jiff."

When the coast was clear, Powell dragged himself to his feet and, moving stiffly, managed to dress in twenty seconds flat. He located the loo down a short hallway, and when he emerged five minutes later, looking half-civilized, Jill was laying their breakfast on a tiny table in the kitchen, complete with a vase of cut flowers. She looked fresh and vibrant as she bustled purposefully about, contrasting markedly with Powell's present state of being. Her long brown hair was tied back and she wore a loose blue jumper.

"You'll make someone a good wife," Powell remarked dangerously.

She smiled sweetly. "You'll be doing the washing up, don't you worry."

Powell pulled a face and gulped down his coffee. "Bloody marvelous," he sighed as Jill refilled his cup. "You don't know how hard it is to get a decent cup of coffee in London."

"I get the beans at Starbucks in Shaftesbury Avenue. It reminds me of home, I guess." There was a hint of something in her voice.

They ate in silence, Powell feeling a little self-conscious. "In case you're wondering," he said eventually, "I don't make a habit of sleeping in strange beds."

"Of course you don't." She hesitated. "But you should look after yourself. I mean, what would your wife think?"

What indeed? he wondered.

She suddenly looked embarrassed. "I-I'm sorry—it's none of my business. I'm beginning to sound like my mother."

Powell smiled ruefully. "Think nothing of it, Jill. I'm well aware of my frailties, believe me."

The tension released, Jill laughed. "You were certainly in good form last night."

Powell had no idea what she was talking about and decided it would be best not to ask. He was dying for a cigarette and tried to suppress the urge. He anointed another piece of toast with marmalade. "Er, any plans for the weekend?"

"Nothing special. My boyfriend's away at his parents' place in the country. I'll probably stick fairly close to home. I've got to work tonight."

"Where do his parents live?"

"In Shropshire somewhere. From what I hear, they own half the county."

"Oh?" Powell remarked significantly.

"I suppose you're wondering why I didn't go with him?"

"The thought never crossed my mind," he lied.

She hesitated. "What the hell? I could use a little fatherly advice. Stephen's parents wanted him to go to Oxford, so they're not happy about him being in London in the first place."

"A highly overrated institution," Powell observed.

"And I get the impression that I don't quite come up to their standards."

"What does Stephen think about all this?"

"I think he's fond of me . . ."

"*Fond* of you?"

She sighed. "Sometimes I wonder if we're really right for each other." Her eyes met his. "Tell me, Powell, what would *you* do if you were in my shoes?"

"Change, as ye list, ye winds; my heart shall be the faithful compass that still points to thee."

Jill looked thoughtful. "Follow my heart, you mean?"

"Something like that."

She looked at him with a quizzical expression. "How did you ever become a cop, anyway?"

"That, my girl, is a long story. I'll tell you about it over the washing up."

Half an hour later, they stood on the doorstep of her flat for an awkward moment. "Thank you, Jill. You've been very kind. I'd like to repay you in some way . . ."

Her eyes twinkled. "Don't be silly. You already have. Now, hurry or you'll miss your train. I'll see you at the pub."

Powell waved as he stepped from the mews into Gower Street. He stopped to light a cigarette, contemplating a jolly weekend spreading manure.

CHAPTER 3

He sat smoking a joint in his bed-sit in King's Cross. The tiny room was littered with clothing, books, and dirty dishes. The place smelled of damp and stale semen. The one small window looked out on the vast tract of desolate ground north of the railway station. A radio blared tinnily somewhere.

He stared at the blank page on the table in front of him. He tried to concentrate, to translate the jumbled images in his head into words on paper, but nothing happened. Turn off that frigging radio, have to think, have to write, he thought, growing increasingly agitated. He knew they wanted him to come crawling back mother father frigging teachers can't make a living writing that crap be sensible for God's sake—"Sod them all!" he screamed, throwing the notebook against the wall. One of the pages came loose and drifted crazily to the floor like a stricken butterfly.

He sat immobile for several minutes, letting his mind drift. You can't force the creative process, he told himself, just need to give it a rest, that's all. Think about something else. He had a girl, hadn't he? That was all that really mattered. He thought about her long brown hair and slim body and fantasized about what he'd like to do to her. His eyes were faraway now. He knew that she barely knew he existed, didn't understand what he was about, but he had a plan to change all that, something so breathtaking in its conception that she would have no choice but to take notice. Then he would have her all to himself. He sucked on the joint again, fingers trembling, and held it in for a long time. He exhaled slowly, watching the smoke drift and curl into spiral clouds illuminated by the shafts of golden light streaming through the window.

It was a typical night at the Fitzrovia Tavern. The kind of night in late April when a raw wind off the North Sea sweeps down Charlotte Street, impelling both the virtuous and the not-so-virtuous to seek refuge in the nearest pub. There was the usual crowd in attendance, and as Jill Burroughs worked behind the bar, mechanically drawing pints and mixing drinks, she realized for the first time since she had been in London that the novelty was beginning to wear off. And now that she thought about it, the sentiment applied equally to her boyfriend, her job, and even to her decision to travel before going back to university. She was in a rotten mood, she couldn't deny it—

There was a loud commotion in the front of the bar. "Did he think he could fob me off like I was a tourist from a coach?" roared a large red-faced man with a perfectly coifed mane of white hair who was holding forth at a crowded table by the window. "When I demanded to know how he could serve such filth, the bloody Frog had the cheek to ask me to leave. When he reads my review on Sunday, he'll know who he's dealing with, by God! It'll be bloody Agincourt all over again!" As the table erupted in laughter, Clive Morton, restaurant critic and self-styled bon vivant fixed his eyes on Jill. "Pull me old handle again, would you, love?" he called out.

"Pull it yourself," she muttered under her breath as she filled another glass with beer. Or, better yet, she thought, get one of your minions to do it for you. Celia Cross, the proprietor of the Fitzrovia, had told her to watch out for Morton when he had arrived a little over an hour ago. The word was he'd been banned from his drinking club in Dean Street and was now reduced to performing for the plebs. He had come in alone and appeared at first to be waiting for someone. It wasn't long, however, before he was joined by a crowd of hangers-on. Jill recognized a couple of media types and one or two others whom she couldn't place but who looked vaguely familiar. Clive Morton clearly reveled in being the center of attention. Jill plonked the glass down on the bar.

"You're not going to make me *come* over there, are you, love?" he asked loudly.

"That'll be one-sixty-five, please," Jill said frostily.

"You'll have to train her better than that, Clive," someone quipped.

Morton got unsteadily to his feet and lurched over to the bar. He scattered a handful of change in Jill's direction. "You should be nicer to me. I could do things for you, y'know." He leered unpleasantly.

His eyes seemed unnaturally bright and his manner was infused with a slightly manic quality that Jill suspected was fueled by more than alcohol. She glared at him. "What did you have in mind exactly?"

"Show you a bit of the good life. For starters."

"And what's for *afters*—me?"

He smirked. "Don't flatter yourself, love."

"Will there be anything else?" she said between clenched teeth.

Morton's eyes narrowed. "You'll be the first to know, I promise you." He picked up his glass and made his way back to his table, spilling beer on the carpet as he went.

As Jill turned to get a bag of crisps for another customer, she sensed someone's eyes on her back. She turned slowly around. He was sitting by himself at his usual table in the corner, staring at her. When he realized he had been caught in the act, he got visibly flustered and started scribbling in the notebook he always carried with him.

The pasty-faced young man with the curly black hair (Jill thought of him as "the Poet") obviously had a crush on her. He came in two or three nights a week for a couple of hours and pretended not to watch her. Whenever she served him, he seemed extremely self-conscious, to the point of incoherence, barely able to string two words together. One night when she was clearing his table, she'd found a crumpled sheet of paper he had left behind. It was a love poem of sorts, or at least a painful attempt at one. More disconcerting was its explicitly erotic content, because she had no doubt it was intended for her. She supposed he was harmless enough, not some sort of deranged stalker or anything like that, but it was beginning to wear on her nerves. She wondered if she should have kept the poem, as evidence or something . . . With an effort she forced her mind off this train of thought. I'm just being silly, she chided herself. She started at the sound of her name.

"Jill, love, you're as white as a sheet! You're not sickening are you?" It was Celia Cross, her employer.

Jill smiled wanly. "Just got a bit of a headache, that's all. I'll be all right."

"That one's not bothering you, is 'e?" The publican threw a disgusted glance at Clive Morton's table.

Jill grimaced. "Don't worry, I'm used to his type. I—" She was about to explain about the Poet but decided it could wait for a better time. Her head had begun to pound now, to the point where she could hardly think straight.

Celia examined her from head to toe, an expression of fond concern on her face. "Look, love, why don't you go 'ome and get a good night's sleep—do you a world of good," she pronounced, having made her diagnosis. "Raymond and I can manage."

"Thanks, Celia. I'll make it up next week."

"Don't be silly. Now off you go," she admonished.

A few minutes later, Jill was walking home down Windmill Street. The darkened street, lined with shops and art galleries, was deserted at this time of night, and she felt vaguely uneasy. She paused, shivering convulsively. I'm probably just coming down with a bug, she told herself. She started walking again, fixing her attention on the streetlamp lighting the corner up ahead. In the distance, she could see the lights of the traffic in the Tottenham Court Road. It had started to rain, so she began to hurry. She stopped in the reassuring pool of light beneath the streetlamp and looked up at the rain slanting like silver tinsel against the sky and began to open her umbrella. Suddenly she froze.

There was a staccato burst of footsteps behind her. *Click click click click click.* Then silence except for the hissing of the rain. For an instant, as the adrenaline surged through her body, she was unable to move, not daring to look around. Then she whirled, brandishing her umbrella, staring wildly into the darkness. She blinked helplessly, her eyes dazzled by the light. She felt like a deer caught in a lorry's headlamps, which was hardly the impression she was trying to create. She thought about calling out, but incongruously, though she was frightened half to death, she didn't wish to appear foolish. Perhaps it had been someone in the next street or someone out for an innocent stroll.

She took a deep breath and was about to continue on her way when she heard it again. It was unmistakable this time—the measured sound of footsteps on pavement, louder now and getting steadily closer. She stared, mesmerized, as a figure emerged from the darkness, casting a long shadow on the rain-slicked street. She heard her own voice. "Who's there?"

The figure kept coming. Without thinking, she threw

her umbrella at her pursuer and watched it clatter harmlessly on the pavement a few feet in front of her. She
turned and ran up the side street then veered left into
Colville Place, which led back to Charlotte Street. Her
heart was pounding in her ears and her lungs felt as if
they were going to burst. The narrow street was lined on
both sides with tall Georgian houses, some with glowing curtained windows that seemed to her now as remote as distant galaxies. She debated for an instant
whether to try pounding on one of the doors to raise help
or to make a dash for it. The sight of her pursuer turning
the corner behind her settled the matter, but at that instant her right foot caught the raised edge of a flagstone
and she fell sprawling to the pavement.

The wet stone was cold on her face. She felt a sharp
pain in her left side, and she couldn't breathe. She could
see a couple passing by on Charlotte Street just ahead.
She tried to cry out but could only gasp for air. She managed to struggled to her feet and began to jog stiffly,
clutching her side, not daring to look back. She could
hear a man's excited voice behind her now.

With a final burst of energy, she turned the corner and
ran across Windmill Street, nearly colliding with a man
carrying a cane who was standing outside the Fitzrovia.

"Sorry," she mumbled breathlessly as she dashed into
the pub.

CHAPTER 4

Powell sat in his office Monday morning reviewing the Brighton file. As Detective-Sergeant Black had suggested in the pub, the case did have its points of interest. On the evening of March 11, at approximately nine-thirty in the evening, one Edith Smith of Number 134 Jamaica Road SE16 was searching for her dog at Butler's Wharf, Bermondsey. Upon hearing a commotion, she observed a man attempting to climb out of the Thames. She was unable to provide assistance, and the man fell back into the river where he is presumed to have drowned. She reported the matter to the local police at Southwark Police Station. At ten-forty-three the same evening, a man's body was recovered from the Thames along the Bermondsey Wall. There was no identification found on the body. The constable attending the scene recognized the deceased and identified him as Richard Brighton, a Labour councillor on Southwark Council, who resided nearby at Number 42 Cardamom Court. When Brighton's spouse, Helen Brighton, returned home just before midnight, she was met by police and taken to the mortuary to view the body, where she confirmed the ID. The results of the postmortem, conducted on the morning of March 12 at ten o'clock, indicated a blunt force trauma to the head inflicted by an unknown object. The actual cause of death was drowning. The coroner concluded that Brighton's death was a homicide perpetrated by a person or persons unknown, possibly during the course of a robbery. Reading between the lines, Powell got the impression that the investigating officer, an Inspector Boles, was not entirely satisfied with this finding. Brighton was thirty-five years old, married, without children, and a schoolteacher by profession, Boles had added as if by way of an afterthought.

Powell was trying to find the pathologist's report amidst the chaos of paper on his desk when Detective-Sergeant Black walked into his office.

"A Miss Burroughs on the phone for you, sir."

Powell frowned. He was still feeling a bit sheepish about Friday night. "I'm up to my neck in it right now. Take her number and tell her I'll ring her back. And come back when you're done, would you?"

"Yes, sir."

Black soon reappeared.

"Sit down, Bill. I was about to have a look at the pathologist's report. Have you seen it?"

The burly sergeant nodded. "Er, I think it's that one beside the ashtray—the stapled one there, sir."

Powell grunted and retrieved it. He skimmed through the report, his face expressionless. When he had finished, he lit a cigarette. He looked speculatively at Detective-Sergeant Black. "It seems straightforward enough."

"Yes, sir," Black replied dutifully.

"I'd like you to review all of the statements and let me know if anything needs following up. And dig up what you can on that property development scheme in Rotherhithe that Brighton was so keen on. I remember seeing him on television a few months ago, attempting to rationalize the number of council tenants that would have to be evicted. Not exactly the way to win a popularity contest, as you so perceptively pointed out. And while you're at it, I'd like a list of the names and phone numbers of the other members of Southwark Council."

Black nodded. "Right."

Powell spent the remainder of the day attempting, without success, to get on top of his backlog of paperwork. When he could take it no longer, around four o'clock, he rang Jill Burroughs. There was no answer.

Two hours later, Powell was in Shad Thames, a narrow cobbled lane that ran behind the refurbished warehouses of Butler's Wharf. Enclosed on both sides by high brick walls crisscrossed with iron walkways, which were used at one time by porters for carrying all manner of goods back and forth, the street was now lined with estate agencies, trendy shops, and a Pizza Express. It was hard to imagine the sinister setting where Bill Sykes had met his end.

Walking out onto the quay, Powell retraced the steps that Edith Smith took on the night of March 11. It was a fine spring morning and a number of people were strolling along the front. He continued east past the Design Museum until he stood in front of the derelict warehouse. He walked over to the railing and looked down into the Thames as the elderly woman had done. Today, however, there was just the usual flotsam to speculate about. He crossed St. Saviour's Dock into Mill Street and soon located Cardamom Court, a converted warehouse with shops and offices on the ground level and flats above.

He rang the bell of Number 42. "Mrs. Brighton? Chief Superintendent Powell."

The lock clicked open, and Powell took the lift to the fourth floor. He was met at the door by an attractive woman in her thirties with short dark hair and sad eyes.

A fleeting smile passed her lips. "Please come in."

"Thank you for agreeing to see me on such short notice, Mrs. Brighton. I'll try not to take up too much of your time."

"I don't suppose a drink would be appropriate under the circumstances. How about a cup of tea?"

Powell smiled. "Lovely."

While Mrs. Brighton was in the kitchen, Powell took in his surroundings. The flat was airy and spacious, with a fine view through the French windows of the north bank of the Thames and the City beyond. The overall impressions created by the pastel decor and modern furnishings were understatement and good taste.

Mrs. Brighton soon returned carrying a tray with the tea things and a plate of biscuits. She placed them on the coffee table and sat down beside him on the settee.

Powell helped himself to a chocolate digestive while she poured. "Lovely view," he commented.

"It is, isn't it? Sugar? We bought in the early Nineties when prices were still affordable. I don't know how young couples just starting out manage these days. I—" Her voice trembled. "I'm sorry, Chief Superintendent."

Powell replaced his cup on its saucer. "Please don't be. I know this is difficult for you, Mrs. Brighton. I'll come directly to the point. As I mentioned to you on the telephone, I've been asked to look into your husband's case, and I want you to know that I will do everything in my power to get to the bottom of it."

She looked at him with an odd expression on her face. "You're still treating it as a robbery, I assume."

"That's the working hypothesis."

"Yes—yes, of course. I thought that you might have meant something else, that's all."

"Something else?"

"Not a robbery, I mean."

He looked at her sharply. "What did you have in mind, Mrs. Brighton?"

She hesitated. "I don't know what I'm thinking half the time, Chief Superintendent." That seemed to be that.

"Would you mind if I asked you a few questions? I'll try to be brief."

"No, of course not."

"Did your husband give an indication of any plans he may have had on the night he died?"

"I can't remember him mentioning anything. We had dinner together here at the flat, then I went out around seven."

"Do you mind me asking where you spent the evening?"

"Not at all. It was Thursday, my girls' night out. I get together with some friends once a week for a glass of wine."

"I see. So it wasn't until you got home that you learned of your husband's death?"

"Yes."

"What time was that?"

"Sometime after eleven-thirty."

"Mrs. Brighton, I'd like you to think carefully about my next question before you answer . . ." He paused for a moment to give her time to consider.

She nodded.

"How would you describe your husband's state of mind that night? You mentioned you had dinner together. Did he act normally? Did he seem to have something on his mind? Was he upset about anything?"

"That's more than one question, Chief Superintendent."

He smiled thinly. "I should have been a barrister."

She seemed to relax slightly. "Let me try and think . . . No, I can't say I remember anything out of the ordinary. I mean, Richard always had a lot on his mind, with council business and so on. But I don't recall him mentioning anything in particular that night."

"He didn't seem despondent or depressed?"

She gave him a penetrating look. "What exactly are you driving at, Chief Superintendent? Are you suggesting that Richard jumped off a bridge or something?"

"I'm not suggesting anything, Mrs. Brighton."

Her eyes flashed angrily. "My husband was a fighter—

he would never have taken his own life. No matter how difficult things got."

"I'm sorry, Mrs. Brighton. I didn't mean to upset you."

She sighed. "I understand, of course. You're just doing your job."

Better to get the worst over with, he thought. "Mrs. Brighton, your husband's body was discovered not far from here. Do you know why he might have gone out that night, where he might have been going?"

She looked at him, eyes moist. "We often went for walks together beside the river. Sometimes he'd go alone."

"Thank you, Mrs. Brighton. I won't take up any more of your time. You've been most helpful. I'll let you know as soon as I have anything to report."

"Yes, well, thank you, Chief Superintendent." She looked slightly disappointed.

As he walked back to London Bridge Station, Powell puzzled over Mrs. Brighton's reaction to his question about her husband's state of mind. She seemed to have jumped to the conclusion that he was alluding to the possibility of suicide, which was rather curious under the circumstances. He thought about what she had said. *My husband was a fighter—he would never have taken his own life. No matter how difficult things got.* He couldn't help wondering what exactly she had meant by "difficult."

CHAPTER 5

When Powell arrived at New Scotland Yard the next morning after a marathon evening spent potting chrysanthemum cuttings, the office was buzzing with the news. Clive Morton, the well-known restaurant critic, had been found with his throat cut in a Soho alleyway earlier that morning. Motivated by an irresistible sense of curiosity, Powell rang his old friend Tony Osborne, Superintendent of Operations at the West End Central Police Station.

"Erskine, old son, to what do I owe this honor?"

"I hear you're having a busy morning."

"Word spreads fast. I can only assume that's a veiled reference to the late Clive Morton, Esquire. What's your interest in the matter, might I ask?"

"I read his column once."

Osborne sighed heavily. "Well, it's a fruity one, I can tell you that much. Morton's body was discovered at approximately six A.M. by a fruit-and-veg lorry driver delivering in Cranbourn Street. The bloke ducked into the alley for a smoke and found him. He'd been beaten about the head, then had his throat cut. According to the constable who attended the scene, the manner of preparation left something to be desired, but the presentation was quite superb."

"I don't follow—"

"He had an apple shoved in his mouth."

"What?"

"You heard me. Whoever did him obviously had a sense of humor."

"Hysterical. Any suspects?"

"Half the restaurateurs in London, I should imagine."

"Was there any sign of robbery?"

"He had his wallet and a considerable quantity of cash on him."

"Did the scene-of-crime lads come up with anything interesting?"

"Negative . . . Erskine, you don't know anything about this business, do you? I'm beginning to get suspicious."

"Just curious. Thanks, Tony. I'd better let you get back to it."

"Right, cheers, mate." Osborne sounded unconvinced.

At least the corpse wasn't marinated in tandoori spices, Powell thought after he had rung off. His macabre musings were interrupted by the arrival of Detective-Sergeant Black, who dumped a thick sheaf of newspaper clippings on his desk. He had obviously been doing his homework.

"What have you got?" Powell asked.

"Well, sir, you've probably read or heard most of this before, so I'll run through it fairly quickly. About a year ago, a development company put forward a proposal to Southwark Council to convert a derelict warehouse on the Thames in Rotherhithe into a block of luxury flats. The proposal also included the development of a commercial complex—shops, restaurants, a recreation center, and so on—across the road on property owned by the borough. The problem is the scheme would require the demolition of a block of council flats. About one hundred tenants would have to be evicted. The developer has argued that the commercial area is essential to the economic viability of the project and has offered to purchase the council-owned land. Based on the current market value of the property, the borough stands to make about ten million quid from the deal."

"I'm sure they'll divide it up amongst the evicted tenants," Powell observed acidly.

"There has been quite a debate about the project," Black continued, "and the council seems to be split about fifty-fifty, which is a bit surprising when you think about it."

"How so?"

"Well, sir, Southwark Council is dominated by Labour—thirty-five Labour councillors, twenty-four Lib Dems, three Conservatives, and two others," he added with customary efficiency and without referring to his notes. "You would have thought—"

"That New Labour has a monopoly on virtue?" Powell interjected. "About the only difference between them and the others is they're better bloody salesmen. The average person's inclination when they got screwed by Mrs. Thatcher was to take to the streets—when you get done by this lot you want to thank them for making you a better person."

Black flushed. "Excuse me, sir, I didn't mean to—"

"Don't mind me. Perhaps I'll start my own party, take up the torch from Screaming Lord Such. Anyway, carry on. I'm finding this most interesting."

Black cleared his throat. "Yes, sir. Moving on to Richard Brighton's role in the matter: He was a supporter from the start, arguing that economic development of this kind was good for the borough in the long term. He took a fair bit of heat over it, but he was generally popular with his constituents and was influential on council. He was also odds-on favorite to be elected the next mayor by his peers."

"What's the present status of the Rotherhithe development?"

"It hasn't come up for a vote yet."

Powell sighed. "I think we're grasping at straws, Bill."

Black got to his feet. "I'm going to keep poking around, if it's all right with you, sir."

Powell nodded absently. When he was alone, he sat smoking for several minutes. Then he picked up the telephone and placed a call to Sir Reginald Quick. He left a message on the pathologist's answerphone.

That evening as Powell walked down Charlotte Street on his way to the Fitzrovia, he found to his considerable irritation that he was unable to keep his mind off the Brighton case. Detective-Sergeant Black had no doubt planted the seed, but a tendril of doubt had begun to grow and take hold. At one level it seemed entirely straightforward. A man out walking alone at night is accosted by a mugger. A struggle ensues and the victim is struck on the head. It was the next step in the sequence of events that didn't sit right. From all appearances, the assailant then chucked his victim into the Thames to drown. Rather vicious behavior for your garden-variety thief. Such things happened of course, but they usually involved drug deals gone wrong or crimes of passion in which the individuals involved were known to each other. The more he thought about it, the more muddled he became.

It was in this pensive state of mind that he wandered into the Fitzrovia. Celia Cross was behind the bar.

Powell looked around. "Jill not working tonight?"

The publican looked worried. "She was supposed to start an hour ago," she said as she filled Powell's glass. "It's not like Jill to be late, Mr. Powell. I rang 'er flat but 'er boyfriend said she wasn't 'ome. I don't know what to think."

"I shouldn't worry too much. She'll probably turn up in a few minutes." He tried to sound reassuring.

She brushed a strand of blonde hair off her forehead with the back of her hand. "Normally I'd agree with you, but what with Saturday night and all . . ."

"Saturday night?"

She looked at him with an odd expression on her face. "I don't suppose you've 'eard, 'ave you?"

"Heard what?"

" 'Ere, you'd better come round the back. Bring your pint with you, and I'll pour meself a nip of gin."

Celia Cross had presided over the Fitzrovia Tavern since her husband died some twenty years ago. A large woman in her fifties who looked ten years younger, she possessed both boundless energy and a good-humored acceptance of the human condition and was quite capable, as she had proven on more than one occasion, of physically removing undesirables from her premises.

That night, however, she looked her age as she sat in her cluttered office with Powell. Unpaid invoices, lists of reminders, and pay sheets papered the surface of her desk. A woman after my own heart, Powell thought.

"Jill said she was going to ring you," Celia said.

Powell remembered the phone call yesterday morning. "I've been, er, busy," he said guiltily.

"It 'appened Saturday night," she began. "Jill was looking poorly, so I sent her 'ome early. Somebody followed her and scared the poor girl half to death. A bleedin' stalker! She ran back 'ere and I called the police, but by the time they got 'ere, the bloke was long gone." She tossed him a disgusted look.

"Any idea who it might have been?"

"Jill thinks it might be an odd bird who comes in 'ere fairly regular—fancies 'imself a writer, apparently. 'E hasn't been back since," she added significantly. "The constable said to let 'im know if 'e shows 'is face in 'ere again."

"I take it this chap was here on Saturday night then."

She nodded.

Powell had slipped unconsciously into the role of detective. "Did anything out of the ordinary take place between them?"

"Not that I can remember, but . . ." She suddenly frowned.

"What is it?"

"Well, Mr. Powell, there was something, but it didn't involve 'im."

"Oh, yes?"

"It was that bloke what got murdered last night. Clive Morton."

This caught Powell's attention. "Really. What happened?"

She screwed up her face as if she had just swallowed something nasty. " 'E was bothering Jill and generally making a nuisance of 'imself. Not behaving like a gentleman, if you get my meaning."

"A shame about Morton," Powell observed.

"You won't see me shedding any tears," the publican pronounced emphatically.

Powell thought for a moment. "If Jill doesn't turn up in the next hour or so, you'd better inform the local police."

She nodded somberly.

As Powell sat in the pub nursing his pint, he could not suppress a growing sense of unease.

CHAPTER 6

Powell sat in Merriman's office the next day being subjected to the Assistant Commissioner's "advice"—a dressing-down, in police parlance.

Merriman's face was red and his eyes bulging. "You must be a complete bloody idiot, Powell. The girl's boyfriend reported her missing last night, and it comes to light that you stayed at her flat on Friday night!"

"There is a perfectly reasonable explanation—" Powell began, sounding defensive in spite of himself.

"Sleeping with a girl half your age is hardly a reasonable explanation." Merriman was sneering now. "I know your type, Powell. You're a bloody disgrace."

Powell had to resist the urge to leap over the desk and throttle his superior. "With the greatest respect, sir, I did not sleep with her, and, in any case, what I do on my own time is my own business," he said in a carefully controlled voice.

"Well, she's gone missing now, hasn't she?"

"Apparently she was followed from the pub on Saturday night—"

"What's it got to do with you?" Merriman snapped. "Look, Powell, if there's anything untoward going on here, I'll have you on the dab so bloody fast your head will spin. In fact I'm going to make it my life's work. Now get out."

Powell did not remember storming out of Merriman's office nor slamming the door behind him. Eyes fixed straight ahead, he brushed past Detective-Sergeant Black, who wisely refrained from saying a word, and secluded himself in his office. He spent the next hour chain-smoking and considering his options. Then he made a decision and rang Tony Osborne.

"Tony, this is strictly on the q.t., right?"

"What's up?"

Powell explained about Jill Burroughs and Merriman.

"That's the trouble with living in commuterland," Osborne said disapprovingly. "Whenever *I* have a snootful, I simply stagger home to my garret in Soho, easy as you please."

"The thing is, Tony, I know your lads are looking into the girl's whereabouts, but I'd like to do a bit of poking around on my own. It's something I feel I need to do."

There was only a moment's hesitation. "Be my guest, mate, only you didn't hear that from me. And you're on your own hook, right?"

"Of course."

"By the way, Erskine, I'm off to Spain for a fortnight starting Sunday. Why don't you stay in my flat—look after things while I'm away. You might find it, er, a little more convenient as a base of operations."

Powell didn't know what to say. "Let me think about it and get back to you. And thanks, Tony, you're a prince among men."

"Right. Cheerio then, mate."

Powell leaned back in his chair and contemplated the benefits of taking his friend up on his offer. A hiatus in Tony Osborne's flat in Lexington Street might be just what the doctor ordered: a change of scene, a sort of mental holiday. And no bloody weeds to worry about. By way of rationalization, he reckoned that with the time he saved by not having to commute, he could devote another couple of hours to the job each day. Whistling tunelessly, he began sorting through the notes that Detective-Sergeant Black had left on his desk.

Tony Osborne called back later that morning. "I hear through the grapevine that you're working on the Brighton case." He paused. "I see. Then you'd better get your arse down here *toot sweet*, mate."

A half hour later, Powell was sitting in Osborne's Savile Row office. Superintendent Tony Osborne was a big man with very little hair, a flamboyant handlebar mustache, and a mind as sharp as a razor. He had started out as a constable in Soho, eventually graduating to the Drug Squad where he quickly earned a reputation as an eccentric. A common method of passing drugs from buyer to seller on the street is by mouth. Money changes hands, then an intermediary of the opposite sex transfers the drugs to the buyer by means of a rather involved and sloppy bout of tongue wrestling. Not surprisingly, few undercover police officers are keen to take posses- sion of the essential evidence in this manner. Osborne, however, played the game with enthusiasm, to the point of being accused in court by one unfortunate victim of trying to shove the stuff down her throat with his tongue, causing her to cough up the goods as it were.

"I won't beat about the bush, Erskine," Osborne began. "We searched Morton's flat and found this in his safe." He tossed over a brown envelope. "I thought you might be interested."

Powell extracted the contents of the envelope—four or five pages stapled together and several loose sheets— and looked through them. There was a contract of some sort between Morton and an entity called the Dock- side Development Corporation, represented by some- one named Paul Atherton, plus several architectural views of a building complex, a block of flats with a restaurant below. He looked more closely. The restau- rant was called Chez Clive. Morton's revenge, he thought.

"Interesting, don't you think?" Osborne observed neutrally.

"The fact that Morton had delusions of culinary grandeur, you mean?"

Osborne cocked an eyebrow. "I'll make allowances for the fact that you've only just started working on the Brighton case—but doesn't the name Dockside Devel- opment Company cause a bubble to come off the old think-tank?"

Powell sighed. "Get to the point, Tony."

"You could show a little more gratitude, mate. Dockside is the development scheme in Rotherhithe that Richard Brighton was trying to shove down the throats of the good citizens of Southwark."

This caught Powell's attention. "You don't say?"

"Which brings me to my point in asking you to come here. I'd like to bring you in on this one. It's probably a long shot, but there may be a connection to the Brighton murder, which is out of my jurisdiction. At the very least, someone is going to have to look into the possibility, and you are the logical candidate." He paused to give Powell the opportunity to consider his request.

If nothing else, Powell mused, Osborne was a breath of fresh air. Divisional Superintendents were generally reluctant to ask for outside assistance, jealously guarding their egos and territories. Osborne, however, possessed sufficient confidence in his own abilities that he took the view that *his* job was to marshal whatever resources were necessary to get the job done. End of story.

For the first time in a long while, Powell experienced that familiar rush of energy signifying that a case had begun to take hold of him like a drug. There was, however, one cloud on the horizon. Powell looked at Osborne with a straight face. "My fee will be the use of your flat while you're away."

Osborne grinned. "Well, that's it then. Do you want me to fix it with Merriman?"

Powell pulled a face. "If you don't mind, I'd like to keep it unofficial for a few days."

Osborne scrutinized his colleague closely. "All right. As long as it gets sorted out before I leave on Sunday."

"Right," Powell concluded with an air of confidence he didn't feel.

The morning mist was beginning to burn off and a pale smudge of sun overhead presaged a fine day ahead. Powell decided to walk to Leicester Square, where, before leaving the West End Central Police Station, he had arranged to meet the fruit-and-veg merchant who had discovered Clive Morton's body. As he walked along the gray curve of Regent Street, filled with shoppers and shop assistants on their breaks, he realized that he rarely took the opportunity to appreciate the fact that he worked in one of the world's great cities. It was always easy to complain about the traffic, the train service, the latest tasteless redevelopment scheme, the tourists, and of course Lord Archer, but he knew he couldn't live anywhere else. From time to time, he and Marion had toyed with the idea of moving to the country, where he could no doubt find a job with a provincial constabulary and she at a local college. He had to admit that the thought of a small holding somewhere in the country, living the life of a country squire shooting pheasants and thrashing poachers, did have its appeal. But when he really thought about it, it all pointed to more gardening. And he had little enough time now outside of his job.

When Peter and David were younger, he had tried to find time for the important things: teaching them to sail and climb, taking them fishing or on family outings, but the pressures of being a policeman had often intruded. Increasingly in recent years, as his sons had grown up and Marion and he had drifted apart, he wondered if he had been much of a father or husband when it really counted. It is interesting, he thought as he crossed Piccadilly Circus past the motley crowd of Euro-kids congregating around Eros, how one's priorities in life only become clear when it is too late to do much about them.

When he arrived in Cranbourn Street, a white lorry marked HUSSEY AND CROWE, FRUITERERS TO LONDON FOR OVER A HUNDRED YEARS was parked as arranged in front of an Italian cafe on the corner of Charing Cross Road. A young man was leaning against it having a smoke. Powell walked over and introduced himself.

The man grinned, cocky but slightly nervous. "Morning, guv. Michael Hussey at your service."

Powell smiled to put him at ease. "Thank you for agreeing to meet me, Michael. I know you've already spoken to someone about this."

"Think nuffing of it, guv. Always happy to help a copper."

"Right then, why don't you tell me exactly what happened?"

Hussey scratched his head. "Tuesday morning it was, going on five o'clock. I'd just made a delivery to the restaurant 'ere. I stopped to 'ave a smoke. For some reason—I can't explain it really—I decided to stretch me legs up Leicester Court there." He pointed to a side street.

"Right. Lead the way."

Hussey led him to a narrow alley lined with refuse bins. "In 'ere. Over there behind that first bin. I saw a pair of legs sticking out, so I went over to 'ave a closer look. He was sitting down, sort of slumped over, like. At

first I thought 'e was drunk, but then I saw all the blood."
He gulped, eyes wide. "It was 'orrible, guv. Stuck like a
pig, 'e was. Wif a friggin' apple stuffed in 'is mouth!"

CHAPTER 7

A young man opened the door to the flat above the garage in Bloomsbury. "Yes?"

"I'm Chief Superintendent Powell. I called earlier about Jill."

"You'd better come in then," the young man said in an unwelcoming tone. "Sit down—you should know your way around by now."

"Mr. Potter, I—"

"Please get to the point, Chief Superintendent. I have a class in twenty minutes." His voice had a slightly nasal quality, and his manner suggested he was used to giving orders.

Powell couldn't imagine what Jill saw in him. "Look, Stephen, I'm here because I'm concerned about Jill and want to do whatever I can to help find her."

"Guilty conscience, Chief Superintendent?"

Powell fixed him with a penetrating stare. "What's that supposed to mean?"

The young man fidgeted uneasily. "Well, I mean, it's a bit irregular, you staying here and—"

"I am only going to explain this to you once," Powell said coldly, "so I suggest you pay attention. I am a regular patron of the pub where Jill works. Last Friday, I missed my train and she kindly offered to put me up for the night. End of story. The fact that Jill told you about it makes my point."

Powell paused to give Potter the opportunity to respond. There was only a strained silence. "The only thing that's *irregular* about all this, Stephen—that's the word you used, isn't it?—is the fact that your girlfriend is missing, and you don't seem the least bit concerned about it."

"Of course I'm concerned," he protested. "I'm worried sick."

"Then you'd better cooperate, hadn't you?"

He ran his fingers through his hair. "Yes, yes, of course." He looked nervous.

"You were away for the weekend, I understand."

"Yes. I was visiting my parents near Shrewsbury."

"Why didn't Jill go with you?"

A guilty look flickered across his face. "She—she had to work."

"Mummy and Daddy have met Jill before, have they?"

"Yes, as a matter of fact. But I don't see that it's any of your business."

Powell smiled his blandest smile. "Just asking. When did you get back to London?"

"Sunday night, around eight o'clock."

"Jill was here at the time?"

Potter nodded.

"Did she seem all right?"

Defensively: "What do you mean?"

Powell sighed. "I mean, what kind of mood was she in? Was she overjoyed to see you? Did she seem worried about anything? Is that clear enough?"

Potter's eyes narrowed. "I'm not sure I care for your tone, Chief Superintendent. And now that I think of it, Jill said you worked for Scotland Yard—I was under the impression that the local police were handling this."

Better not push too hard, Powell thought. All he needed was for Potter to make a complaint and for Merriman to get wind of it. "Look, Stephen, this can be easy or difficult—it's up to you. Jill has disappeared, and I'm trying to help."

Potter seemed to consider this carefully. "All right, I'm sorry," he said eventually. "I'm sure you can appreciate that I'm a bit stressed out. The fact is Jill and I had a hell of a row when I got home. She told me about you staying here, and I reacted like a jealous fool. Then she accused me of not . . ." He smiled weakly. "Let's just say that things went downhill from there. I ended up sleeping on the sofa. When I woke up the next morning, she was gone. I didn't think anything of it at first. She often went for an early morning walk and a coffee. I had classes all day and didn't get home until quite late—"

"What time was that?" Powell interjected.

"Sixish, I think. I assumed Jill was at work. She didn't come home that night, and I won't say I wasn't worried, but I assumed that she'd just gone off somewhere to think things through after our fight. The first indication I had that anything was wrong was when her boss called from the pub yesterday. She's been gone two days now—it's not like Jill to do something like this, Chief Superintendent."

Powell looked at the young man with a curious expression on his face. "Didn't she tell you about what happened to her Saturday night?"

Potter looked puzzled. "She didn't mention anything. What do you mean?"

"She had a rather harrowing experience, I'm afraid."

"I don't understand."

Powell described Jill's encounter with the stalker on the way home from work.

Potter held his head in his hands. "I had no idea. I've been a bloody fool. I can see that now."

Powell wasn't sure he believed him.

Later, as he crossed the Tottenham Court Road, he couldn't help wondering if things might have turned out differently had he taken Jill's call Monday morning.

It was early yet, and there were only a few other customers in the Fitzrovia. He was greeted by Celia Cross.

She smiled. "Afternoon, Mr. Powell." Then her expression turned serious. "Any word about Jill?"

"I'm afraid not."

She shook her head as she filled his glass. "This is so unlike 'er." She looked at Powell with watery eyes. "I just know something 'as 'appened."

Powell told the publican about Jill's fight with her boyfriend.

Celia rolled her eyes. "That snob! Swans about like Lord Muck. I can't imagine what the girl sees in 'im."

"That was my initial reaction as well, but I think he's genuinely worried about her. The point is she may have gone off for a few days to sort things out. These things happen."

Celia looked doubtful. "I dunno, I just—" Her eyes suddenly widened as if she'd seen a ghost. She grabbed Powell's sleeve. "It's 'im," she whispered, "the writer!"

Powell turned and saw a scraggly looking youth standing in the doorway. Their eyes met for an instant, then the man dropped the package he was carrying and attempted to run out the door. Unfortunately for him, a man weighing about eighteen stone was just coming in. It was a collision of notable effect. The young man bounced back and crashed sprawling into a table and chairs. Powell rushed over, grabbed him by the scruff of the neck and hauled him, struggling weakly, to his feet. His bloodshot eyes stared wildly in his pasty face and he reeked of cannabis. Powell couldn't resist. "Hello, hello, what's all this then? I'm Chief Superintendent Powell. Who are you?"

"Get you h-hands off me, you f-facist pig!" the young man protested.

"An angry young man, by the sound of it, Ms. Cross. Would you mind if I took him down to the Writer's Bar for a little chat?"

Celia Cross smiled carnivorously. "Be my guest, Mr. Powell. You can't 'ear a thing up 'ere."

Powell released his charge. "Pick up your package," he ordered.

"Sod off!"

Powell moved in front of the door and slid it over with his foot. "Pick it up, my lad, or I'll shove it up your bloody arse."

This seemed to catch the young man's attention, and he did what he was told. The package looked to be about nine by twelve by two inches thick, wrapped in grease-stained brown paper and tied with string.

Powell smiled. "That's better. After you." He gestured toward the rear of the pub. "Down the stairs, first door on your left; I'm sure you know the way."

Muttering to himself, the young man shuffled off with Powell following close behind.

CHAPTER 8

The Writer's Bar was a shabby room in the basement of the pub where Dylan Thomas, George Orwell, Ezra Pound, and T. S. Eliot used to come to get plastered. The dark-paneled walls were hung with framed photographs commemorating the bar's former habitués.

Powell turned his attention to the young man's driving license. "Now then, Mr., er, Snavely—or would you prefer I called you Simon?"

There was a sullen silence.

Powell sighed. "All right, Simon. Why don't you tell me about yourself?"

He eyed Powell suspiciously. "Wh-what do you m-mean?"

"You can start by telling me what you do for a living."

"I'm a p-p-poet," he stammered.

Powell raised an eyebrow. "A poet, are you? I enjoy a bit of poetry now and again. What have you written?"

"I haven't actually had anything p-published, but what I d-do is quite experimental." He was sulking now.

And no doubt unreadable as well, Powell thought. "I'm interested in how you keep body and soul together— you know, pay the rent and buy your groceries."

"It's n-none of your f-f-frigging business."

Powell sighed heavily. "I've got all day, Simon." He waited patiently.

Snavely began to fidget in his seat. His hand trembled. "Look," he said, "I need to g-get out of here. Wh-what's this all about anyway?"

Powell considered his disheveled, malodorous charge as if he were something crawling inside a jar—a young man, he surmised, badly in need of a little something to soothe his troubled mind. Powell took out his cigarettes, drew one from the package and lit it with exaggerated precision. He returned the package to his jacket pocket, exhaling slowly. "You haven't answered my question, Simon."

Snavely looked wistfully at the cigarette. "I recite poems on the street c-corner and p-p-pass the hat around, if you m-must know."

"Where are your parents?"

"Birmingham," he mumbled.

"What are you doing in London?"

"I was a s-student at London University for a while. I—I wasn't learning a f-frigging thing, so I . . ." He seemed to lose his concentration.

"So you dropped out to write poetry."

"Yeah, something like that."

Time to change tacks. "I understand you know Jill Burroughs, the barmaid here."

He averted his eyes. "I d-don't actually know her—"

"Oh, I think you do, Simon. I understand that you were here at the pub on Saturday night. Is that right?"

"I m-may have been." His voice was tight, edgy.

"Jill was working that night, wasn't she?"

"W-what of it?" He swallowed hard.

"What time did you leave?"

"Can't remember."

"Do you remember what time you got home?"

He tried to smile. "Sorry. I f-forget things sometimes."

"I'll get straight to the point, Simon. Jill Burroughs hasn't been seen since Monday, and we're starting to get worried about her."

"W-what's it got to do with m-me?"

"That depends, doesn't it, Simon?"

"I don't know what you're t-talking about." There was a look of alarm in his eyes.

"Oh, I think you do, Simon." With a sudden violent motion, Powell slammed his fist down on the table.

Snavely started with a yelp and nearly fell off his chair. "What did y-you do that f-f-for?" he asked indignantly.

"I don't like being messed about," Powell snapped. "Jill told her employer, Ms. Cross, that you tried to follow her home Saturday night. She said you scared the hell out of her."

Snavely's mouth opened and closed soundlessly.

"Fancy yourself a stalker, do you, Simon?"

"You—you d-don't understand!" he managed to blurt out.

"I think it might be best if we searched your flat."

The young man's face grew even paler.

Powell smiled without humor. "You should lay off the ganja, Simon. It'll fry your brain."

Snavely shook his head. "You're wrong—about Jill, I mean. I'd n-never hurt her. I'm in l-love with her."

"What?"

"I followed her because I wanted to g-give her this." He picked up the brown-paper package.

"What's that then?"

"Poems. For her. I've been working on them f-for months."

"Open it."

Snavely laboriously untied the string, then carefully unfolded the wrapping paper, revealing a cardboard box of the type in which writing paper is sold. He removed the lid, withdrew a thick sheaf of paper, and pushed it over.

Powell flipped through the sheets in amazement. There must have been fifty pages, handwritten on both sides. The untidy scrawl was barely legible, but from what he could make out it was a collection of sonnets dedicated to Snavely's true love. They were written in the Shakespearean style and were quite simply the most dreadful drivel he had ever read. And even worse, each sonnet had only twelve lines, the final rhyming couplet having been forgotten apparently. The standard of education these days. He handed the poems back.

"Take my advice, Simon, don't quit your day job."

First thing the following morning, Powell and Black met briefly to compare notes. Powell was a bit on edge, having just avoided bumping into Merriman on his way up. He lit a cigarette. "I've asked Superintendent Os-borne to send over the file on Clive Morton," he said. "It turns out he had a connection with the development scheme in Rotherhithe that got Brighton in hot water." He explained about Chez Clive. "It's a long shot, but we can't afford to rule anything out at this point. I'll concentrate on Morton for the time being; you can get started on Brighton's council colleagues."

Black grinned. "About Mr. Morton, sir, you have to admit the garnish was a nice touch. Maybe somebody didn't like one of his restaurant reviews."

Powell grunted.

"Any word on Miss Burroughs, sir?"

Powell related the events of the previous day at the Fitzrovia Tavern.

"A dead end then, sir?"

Powell shrugged. "Too early to tell. I'll have Snavely's flat searched and we'll see what turns up."

"Thou hast the keys of paradise, oh just, subtle, and mighty opium!" Black intoned solemnly.

Clive Morton's flat was situated in a surprisingly quiet corner of Mayfair just minutes from Oxford Street. Powell located the redbrick mansion block in Binney Street and buzzed himself up. He was met at the door by Morton's housekeeper, a frowsy middle-aged woman with bright red lipstick and a sour demeanor.

"I was just about to leave when my old man rang me and told me to wait for you." she said resentfully.

"I am most grateful, Mrs. Hobson," Powell replied pleasantly. "I'll try not to keep you too long."

"I've 'eard that one before," she grumbled.

Fussy and ostentatious, Morton's flat contrasted sharply with the Brightons'. The sitting room was cluttered with antique furniture in the rococo style, making the space appear smaller than it actually was. Powell selected an elaborately ornate wing chair and sat down. "Do sit down, Mrs. Hobson. I'd like to ask you a few questions about your late employer."

The unsmiling housekeeper parked herself reluctantly on the edge of an embroidered settee opposite. She sat stiffly with her hands folded in her lap.

"Now, then, Mrs. Hobson, you might begin by telling me what you are doing here."

She looked at him as if he were an escapee from a lunatic asylum. "I was tidying up the place—what else would I be doing? Mr. Morton's sister is coming down this weekend to go through 'is things."

"I see. Tell me, Mrs. Hobson, what sort of arrangement did you have with Mr. Morton?"

She frowned. "Arrangement?"

"How often did you come here to clean house?"

"Three afternoons a week. Monday, Wednesday, and Friday."

"Do you have other clients as well?"

She nodded grudgingly.

"How long have you worked for Mr. Morton?"

"Going on ten years now."

"I'm sure this has come as quite a shock to you. When did you first hear that he'd been murdered?"

"Not until I 'eard it on the telly Tuesday evening.

When I was 'ere on Monday afternoon, I saw that 'is bed 'adn't been slept in," she added quickly. "But I didn't think nothing of it."

"Oh?"

She tossed him a knowing look. " 'E often stayed out all night."

"Did he now? Do you know if he had a regular lady friend?"

The housekeeper cackled harshly. "A 'lady friend'? That's a good one, that is! Who'd put up with the likes of 'im? Tell me that."

"What exactly do you mean, Mrs. Hobson?"

She narrowed her eyes. "Very demanding, 'e was, if you get my meaning. You had to know 'ow to 'andle 'im."

Powell detected a note of pride in her voice. "You knew how to handle him, didn't you, Mrs. Hobson?"

"Not 'alf!" she snorted.

"Where do you suppose he was then, on Monday night?"

"Out with some tart, I expect," she replied without hesitation.

Powell raised an eyebrow. "You mean a prostitute, Mrs. Hobson?"

She stared at him. "What else?"

"Did Mr. Morton often consort with prostitutes?"

"Whenever the dirty old sod could get it up, I expect."

Powell suspected that Mrs. Hobson would not be asked to give the eulogy at Morton's funeral.

"Sometimes he'd bring them 'ere," the housekeeper

continued in a conspiratorial tone. "You wouldn't believe the things they'd get up to! I'd 'ave to pick up after them. It was disgusting!"

"The imagination runs wild, Mrs. Hobson. I can't imagine how you put up with it."

Mrs. Hobson lowered her voice. "Once the 'ubby and I were in Leicester Square after the cinema, and we saw Mr. Morton hanging about with all the other punters, chatting up some tart!"

Powell's mental antennae began to vibrate. That would be just a stone's throw from Leicester Court where Morton's body was found. He leaned forward in his chair. "I'll let you in on a little secret, Mrs. Hobson, but only if you promise not to tell anyone. Can I count on you?"

The housekeeper was positively glowing now. "Of course, Chief Superintendent! Mum's the word."

"I'm working on the theory that Mr. Morton was murdered by someone he knew. Can you think of anybody who might have had it in for him?"

She looked skeptical. "You're joking."

"You did say he was very, er, demanding, Mrs. Hobson."

"Yeah, well, I can think of a 'undred people who didn't *like* 'im. *I* didn't like 'im, come to that, but that's a different thing than killing 'im, isn't it?"

"Very true, Mrs. Hobson, very true. But are you sure there isn't someone in particular who may have had a score to settle with him?"

The housekeeper's face tightened into a state of deep concentration as she considered this possibility. For the first time, Powell became aware of a clock ticking loudly somewhere in the house.

"If you ask me," she said eventually, "it was one of 'is bleedin' tarts."

CHAPTER 9

Back at the Yard, Powell sorted through his mail and discovered that the Morton file had arrived from West End Central. He took it with him to the cafeteria where he hoped he could study it free from interruptions. He paid for a cup of the instant swill that passes for coffee in such establishments and selected a table by a window. He was just starting in on the pathologist's report when he sensed somebody standing beside him. He looked up.

It was Detective-Sergeant Sarah Evans, carrying a tray laden with tea things and some sort of seed-infested muffin.

"You don't look very glad to see me," she said brightly.

Powell sighed. "Sit down, Evans. But spare me the chirpiness."

"I hear you're working with Bill Black on the Brighton case," she said as she settled herself across from him.

"Word does get around."

"Are you making any progress?"

"It's early days yet." Powell's eyes rested lightly on her, and he liked what he saw. Bright, capable, and ambitious, not to mention extremely attractive, she had assisted him on the Yorkshire moors murder, proving her mettle on her first major investigation. "What have you been up to?" he asked.

She grimaced. "Not much, I'm afraid. I could use a good murder case to get the juices flowing again."

"I'll keep you in mind."

"Thanks. By the way, I hear Merriman's got it in for you."

"Charming," Powell rejoined. "My life is an open book."

She laughed. "You should be flattered that I'm interested." She poured herself a cup of tea from the miniature pot. "Now then, why don't you tell me all about the case?"

"I was hoping to get some work done," Powell said pointedly.

"Oh, come on. For old times' sake."

"I never could resist your charms, Evans. I will comply with your request if you promise to leave me in peace when I'm finished."

She nodded eagerly, whilst attempting to saw through her muffin with the plastic knife that had been provided.

"About a month ago," Powell began, "Richard Brighton, the Southwark councillor, was found floating in the Thames without his wallet. The locals are treating it as a mugging but haven't been able to come up with any suspects—"

"I remember reading something in the papers about a controversial development that Brighton was involved in—I think it involved the eviction of some council tenants," Evans interjected. "Maybe he had enemies."

"Thank you for jumping in with your ideas, Evans. I find these brainstorming sessions so stimulating."

She smiled innocently, ignoring the sarcasm. "No problem. Two heads are better than one, I always say."

"As *I* was about to say, it may in fact be a case of simply being in the wrong place at the wrong time. However, we are considering other possibilities, including the one you mentioned."

"That's it?"

"That's it."

Evans looked disappointed.

"There is one other thing . . ." Powell said mischievously

"Oh, yes?"

"I expect you've heard about Clive Morton."

"The late restaurant critic."

"The very one. Found with his throat cut in an alley in Soho early Tuesday morning."

Evans looked puzzled. "I don't see the connection."

"The ability to discern patterns and relationships amidst a chaos of clues is the hallmark of a good detective, Evans."

She flushed but didn't say anything.

"By coincidence, it turns out that Morton had a business interest in the very development scheme you alluded to."

"You once told me that you didn't believe in coincidences."

"In this case, I'm not so sure . . . It also seems that Morton had a predilection for ladies of the evening; it may be that one of them didn't appreciate his critical review of her performance."

Evans looked doubtful. "A little drastic, don't you think?"

"You never know—a woman scorned . . ."

She ignored this. "Did he have his wallet on him?"

"You impress me, Evans. Yes, he did, as a matter of fact."

Sarah pondered this for a moment. "I used to read Morton's column occasionally for a laugh. It seems to me that he often referred to a companion—you know, 'my companion had to endure the execrable escargot' sort of thing. It might be interesting to find out who she was and what she thought about his extracurricular activities."

"That's a good point, although his housekeeper maintains that no one would put up with him."

"I'm not surprised." She paused thoughtfully. "If you want my advice, I'd concentrate on Brighton. If there's a connection with the Morton case, that's the place to look."

"Thank you for your advice, Evans. Now then, if you've finished your tea, I really should be getting back to work."

"I can take a hint," she said with good humor. She stood and picked up her tray. "But if you want to bounce any more ideas off me . . ." She trailed off hopefully.

Powell looked at her speculatively. "I just may do that, Evans. What about lunch tomorrow? I seem to recall promising you in Yorkshire that I'd take you to the K2 sometime."

She hesitated only for an instant. "Thanks. I'd like that."

"I'll meet you in the Back Hall at noon tomorrow."

After a slightly awkward moment, she replied, "Right. I'll see you then.

When Evans had gone, he turned once more to the pathologist's report and began humming to himself.

"There's no shortage of bad feelings on the local council, that seems clear enough," Detective-Sergeant Black concluded later in Powell's office. I chatted up the clerk at the council office—a Miss Froy—who was most helpful. She indicated that the councillors basically fall into two camps on the Dockside project— those for it, led by Brighton, and those against it, with no in-between as far as I can tell. She mentioned two individuals in particular. One is a solicitor named Charles Mansfield. He's a Conservative who supports the project but who felt that Brighton was an opportunist trying to hijack the Conservative agenda. Interestingly, Mansfield was also Brighton's chief rival for mayor and was generally considered to be the underdog, given the composition of the council. The other bloke is Adrian

Turner, a Labour activist and the leader of the anti forces who accused Brighton of selling out his socialist principles."

"Sounds like a microcosm of contemporary British politics," Powell observed.

"Yes, sir," Black said tolerantly. "And there's more. The most vocal opponent of the scheme is a woman named Tess Morgan. She represents the tenants of the council block that gets demolished if the project goes ahead. Apparently she's threatened to do whatever it takes to stop it, including lying down in front of the bull-dozers, if it comes to that."

"Keep poking around and see if you can come up with anything else. In the meantime, I'll have a chat with our two political rivals and the community activist."

Black nodded. "Anything new in the Morton case, sir?"

Powell described his conversation with Mrs. Hobson the housekeeper. "It seems old Clive liked to look for love in all the wrong places," he concluded.

"Maybe he got in a dispute with a pimp," Black ventured.

"It's a possibility," Powell agreed. He recalled what Sarah Evans had said and mentioned it to Black. "According to Mrs. Hobson, Morton wasn't involved in a long-term relationship, but we should probably find out who his dinner companions were."

Black frowned. Something was clearly bothering him. "What about Morton's connection with Dockside, sir?"

"I'll follow that up," Powell replied absently. He was thinking about the postmortem report. Something was scrabbling around in a dark corner of his brain.

Helen Brighton picked up the telephone, her hand moving in slow motion. "Yes . . . ? I'm all right, thanks . . . You didn't have to—I've told you, it's too soon. I need time to think . . ." Her voice was reluctant. "He was still my husband . . ." She sighed. "I know you don't."

She closed her eyes as she listened to the sound of his voice, her face expressionless. She could hear the hum of traffic through the open window. She had heard it all before, had even tried to convince herself with the same reasoned arguments. There was no escaping the fact that her life had changed utterly. He was dead now, and she was free to do as she wished. Why shouldn't she think about what *she* wanted for once? His voice was passionate, persuasive, awakening something in her she hadn't felt for a long time. The relationship would have to be on her terms—she could never again be content to simply serve someone else's ambition. She was motivated by something much more basic. She wanted desperately to believe in something again. A sudden cooling breeze pressed the fabric of her dress against her body, and she opened her eyes. She knew there were those who wouldn't understand, who would draw their own conclusions, but she no longer cared what other people thought. There was a silence on the other end of the line. She took a deep breath. "Yes, all right. In twenty minutes." She replaced the receiver in its cradle and sat motionlessly, watching the restless stirring of the curtains.

CHAPTER 10

The next morning, Powell was en route to the Southwark Police Station to see Inspector Boles, the officer
who had been investigating Richard's Brighton's murder.
He had put it off as long as possible, as he could well
imagine how the locals felt about having the rug pulled
out from under them, but it came down to a matter of
common courtesy. And he could not deny that he was
motivated in part by self-interest: It was possible, indeed
likely, that Boles would have something to contribute
that hadn't made its way into the official report.

It was with these thoughts in mind that Powell passed
through the claustrophobic confines of Clink Street,
past the notorious prison of the same name—now a
tourist trap—where color tellies and fitness facilities, or
at least their historical equivalents, would have been
an anathema. It was raining lightly, and he thought
about the umbrella he had left propped in the corner of
his office behind the door. Ahead was the massive stone
tower of Southwark Cathedral, dark and brooding above

a labyrinth of brick warehouses and a hulking, clanking railway viaduct. Powell followed underneath the viaduct to Borough High Street. By the time he got to the police station, he was damp and cold and not in the best of moods.

Inspector Boles, a donnish-looking man with a pallid complexion, didn't look particularly happy to see him, but, to his credit, he was pleasant enough and ushered Powell into a tiny windowless office. After the usual formalities, Powell got straight to the point.

"I won't try to justify the fact that I'm here, Boles, but suffice it to say I had about as much choice in the matter as you did. In any case, here we are."

Boles smiled a paper-thin smile. "Let me put you at ease, Mr. Powell. I've been around long enough to have learned that Lord Tennyson got it about right: *Theirs not to reason why, Theirs but to do and die.* I don't take it personally."

"I'd appreciate your views on this business, Boles. You're much closer to it than I am."

He regarded Powell thoughtfully. "I must admit," he said, "I had mixed feelings about this one from the start. On the one hand, it seemed like a piece of cake. Brighton goes for a walk along the river near his home one night and has the misfortune to encounter someone desperate for a few quid—a junkie perhaps. A struggle ensues, and Brighton is struck on the head. When he realizes what he has done, our assailant panics and pushes his victim over the railing into the Thames. It certainly wouldn't be the first time that sort of thing has happened in Bermondsey. This used to be a pretty rough area—

still is in some parts despite the recent development boom." He paused.

"And on the other hand . . ." Powell prompted.

Boles frowned. "Mention Richard Brighton to anyone in the borough, and you're sure to get a strong reaction one way or the other. People either loved him or hated him. The traditional Labour types accused him of selling his soul to Mrs. Thatcher, the Conservatives were jealous of his success, and the yuppies—who have flocked here in the last few years—loved him. He won his seat on the council by a landslide last election, and he was being touted as the next mayor. And I personally think that his ambition extended well beyond that. He was charismatic and articulate, with an attractive wife who is a successful businesswoman in her own right."

Powell smiled crookedly. "Sounds like your typical Blairite."

"You're right. But in Brighton's case, one got the impression there was a worm in the apple. Even some of his most die-hard supporters felt that he'd gone beyond the pale with the position he'd taken on the proposed Dockside development in Rotherhithe." He looked at Powell with a questioning expression.

Powell nodded. "I know about it.

"Brighton said all the right things, of course," Boles continued. "How the increased revenue would allow the council to provide better services and facilities for the greater good of the people of Southwark." He hesitated, as if searching for the right words. "But it seemed out of character somehow, even for him. Promoting development is one thing, but turning upward of a hundred council tenants out into the street is quite another."

"Do you think," Powell asked carefully, "that someone could be so set against the project he or she would resort to murder?"

Boles's eyes blinked slowly in his pale face. "It beggars the imagination doesn't it? On the other hand, the only thing tying Brighton's murder to a robbery is the fact that his wallet was missing." He looked at Powell. "All I know is my instincts tell me it was something personal."

As Rashid Jamal, clucking like a broody hen, cleared away the dishes from their table, Detective-Sergeant Sarah Evans leaned back in her chair and sighed contentedly. "Mere words cannot do justice to that *korma*."

Rashid flashed a grin. "Thank you, miss. You are most kind."

When they were alone again, Evans regarded Powell speculatively. Because it was ostensibly a social occasion, she felt she could dispense with the usual formalities, although it was admittedly a fine line she was treading. "Although I'm certainly not complaining, you didn't ask me here to discuss the Brighton case, did you?"

Powell smiled thinly. "You'll make a great detective someday, Evans. To answer your question, no I didn't actually. Apart from an excuse to enjoy your company, I wanted your views on another matter. As a woman, I mean."

She looked at him suspiciously, oblivious to his compliment. "What do you mean, 'as a woman'?"

He frowned. "It's about this young friend of mine—more of an acquaintance, really . . . She works at the pub next door . . ." He went on to tell Evans about Jill Burroughs and the events leading up to and following her disappearance.

Evans listened intently. When Powell had finished his account, she thought about it for a moment. "I think you can call her a friend," she said pointedly, "since I take it she wasn't running some sort of doss house in Bloomsbury."

Powell screwed up his face. "Ouch!" he said.

"You know what I mean. She sounds like a very nice person, and I can understand why you're worried. But try and look at things from her point of view."

"What do you mean?"

"It sounds to me like the poor girl had a weekend from hell. I'll leave aside the events of last Friday night and the psychological impact of having a policeman commandeer her couch for the night—"

"Very funny."

"That bloke who was always hanging about the pub watching her—the so-called poet—is obviously completely crackers. It must have worn on her nerves, and when he tried to follow her home that night, it was the last straw."

"So she ran away?" Powell ventured doubtfully.

Evans looked disappointed in him. "She was living away from home in a foreign country, she was being pursued by some screwy sonneteer, and from what you've said, she was involved in an iffy relationship with a young man whose family wasn't thrilled with the idea. And come to think of it, working in a pub can't be all fun and games—having to put up with the Clive Mortons of the world, for instance."

"Yes, well, look what happened to him," Powell said to no one in particular.

Evans shrugged. "Perhaps she just needed to get away for a while to think things through. God knows I wish I could sometimes. Anyway, that's my gut reaction, based on what you've told me."

"But why not tell someone? Her employer for instance."

Evans looked thoughtful. "I think it's the kind of thing one would tend to do on the spur of the moment if one felt really hard-pressed, without necessarily thinking about the consequences."

"There are, of course, more sinister possibilities," Powell said, stating the obvious.

Evans looked at him with her clear blue eyes. "You asked me for my opinion, and I've given it to you. As a woman," she added dryly.

He smiled warmly. "And an exceedingly pleasant luncheon companion, at that. Thank you, Evans. You've been most helpful." His expression turned serious. "And I sincerely hope you're right about Jill."

Powell escorted Detective-Sergeant Evans to the tube station, then, motivated by the need to clear his head, decided to go for a walk alone with no particular destination in mind. He stepped into the Tottenham Court Road under an equivocal gray sky. During the course of his discussion with Evans, he had come to realize on a conscious level just how worried he was about Jill Burroughs. In an irrational way, he felt that he was partly responsible for complicating her life, perhaps even contributing to her decision—if that is in fact what it was—to run away from her problems. And that was the most optimistic scenario; the others didn't bear thinking about. He had been carelessly free with advice that morning in Jill's flat, advice that he had rarely followed in his own life. Follow your bloody heart indeed. He shook his head in disgust. In any case, there was nothing he could do about it now. Time would tell whether Evans's intuition was sound. He found the acceptance of this self-evident fact strangely liberating.

As he walked past the endless line of discount computer and stereo shops, he concentrated his attention on the disparate murders of Richard Brighton and Clive Morton. A popular Labour councillor is found floating in the Thames, an apparent robbery victim. Then, a month later, Clive Morton, the notorious restaurant critic and a thoroughly disagreeable chap by all accounts, has his throat slit in a Soho alley. In Morton's case, there was no indication of robbery; however, the corpse had been garnished with an apple, which was, to say the least, suggestive. Morton had often boasted in his newspaper column that he could make or break a restaurant's reputation, and the sheer number of London restaurateurs who were the victims of a scathing review, and who would no doubt have taken great pleasure in personally administering the coup de grâce, boggled the mind. At this point, Powell had to suppress a mental image of a maniacal Rashid Jamal furtively feeding his tandoor.

At the corner of New Oxford Street, a green-glass and concrete office tower dominated the skyscape like an obscene finger. Powell turned into the nearest pub. The only apparent similarity in the two crimes, he mused as he sipped his beer, was the fact that both men had been initially struck on the head before being dispatched in dramatically different ways. On the surface of it then, here were two unrelated events: one a random act of violence of the type so prevalent nowadays, the other something more personal perhaps. There was, however, one potential fly in this particular ointment and without a doubt the most intriguing revelation in the case so far: Clive Morton's connection—via his proposed restaurant, Chez Clive—with the Dockside development scheme in Rotherhithe, the very same scheme on which Richard Brighton had staked his political future.

As he watched the steady stream of passersby on the pavement outside, it occurred to him that his approach up until now had been hit-and-miss. Even Black had politely made the point. It was time to sweep the personal clutter from his mind and get down to business. He drained his pint, then reached into his pocket for his mobile phone.

CHAPTER 11

Forty-five minutes later, Powell found himself once again in Shad Thames. The office he was looking for was sandwiched between a gourmet food shop and a clothing boutique. P. K. ATHERTON, PROPERTY DEVELOPERS AND ESTATE AGENTS the sign in the window proclaimed discreetly. Powell announced himself to the secretary, a smashing young redhead with green eyes who invited him in a lilting brogue to take a seat while she went to inform Mr. Atherton. Presently he could hear the murmur of voices.

A few minutes later, she returned to escort him through a door at the rear of the main reception area. There was no sign of any other employees. At the end of a short hallway, she ushered him into a large office that was sparsely furnished with a few good pieces of furniture (to give an impression of richness, he surmised) in addition to the usual file cabinets and office paraphernalia. A man about his age, fit-looking in a short-sleeved white shirt, tie loosened casually, sat behind a massive desk. He smiled and stood up, extending his hand across the desk. "Paul Atherton," he said as they shook hands. He gestured for Powell to sit down in a green leather–upholstered chair across from him. "Please shut the door, Ms. Kelly, and hold my calls."

Powell discreetly surveyed his surroundings as he took his seat. There was a closed door to his right. Mounted on the oak-paneled wall behind his host was a small glass cabinet, inside of which was displayed a pair of antique percussion dueling pistols in their fitted, baize-lined case. On the corner of the desk was a Christie's auction catalogue of antique arms that one suspected had been strategically placed to look as if it had been tossed there casually.

Atherton noticed Powell's apparent interest. "You aren't a collector, by any chance, are you, Chief Superintendent?" he asked.

Powell smiled. "You should see my basement."

Atherton laughed unselfconsciously. "The desire to acquire things, whether one needs them or not, is an innate human characteristic, I fear. I've long ago given up trying to fight it." His expression suddenly became sober. "Now, then, what exactly can I do for Scotland Yard?"

"As I mentioned on the telephone, I was hoping you could answer some questions I have about your proposed development on the Thames in Rotherhithe. I'll try not to take up too much of your time."

Atherton frowned. "Not at all, Chief Superintendent, although I can't see that I'll be of much help to you. I find it inconceivable that Richard Brighton's death had anything to do with Dockside."

"I admit it's a long shot, but if I can eliminate it as a possibility, my job will be that much easier."

Atherton seemed satisfied with this response. "What do you want to know?" he asked.

"I understand that Dockside tends to arouse the passions of both its supporters and detractors," Powell replied tactfully. "Perhaps you could begin by giving me a bit of background on the project."

Atherton shook his head ruefully. "It never ceases to amaze me how people who claim to have the best interests of their community at heart can consistently stand in the way of progress and not see the hypocrisy of their position. Times change—that's the nature of things and it's futile to deny it. At one time, London boasted the largest enclosed cargo dock system in the world. Each dock was surrounded by forty-foot-high walls and set up for a specific type of cargo. They even had their own police forces. With the advent of container ships in the Sixties, however, everything changed. Freighters that took a fortnight to unload using traditional methods were being replaced with container ships that could be turned around in twenty-four hours. In addition, much of the cargo that used to be transported by rail through London to the docks was now being carried on truck ferries plying to and from Europe. To make a long story short, the port moved downriver, and the docks closed one by one. One can mourn the loss of a way of life, but one cannot turn back the clock, Chief Superintendent."

Powell grunted neutrally.

"Essentially, we're talking about five thousand acres of land, seven hundred acres of water, twenty miles of riverfront, and hundreds of buildings that no longer served a useful purpose," Atherton continued with growing enthusiasm. "In the Seventies and Eighties, Docklands, as we now know it, was a wasteland of abandoned warehouses with high unemployment and a dwindling population, but it was the development opportunity of a lifetime for those with the vision to see it. The renaissance, if I may put it that way, began with Canary Wharf. Despite a temporary setback due to the nineteen-ninety recession, which pleased the naysayers no end," he added with a hint of contempt in his voice, "Canary Wharf alone now provides nearly five million square feet of high-quality office space, very little of it vacant. And there is a growing demand for residential properties as well. Prices here in Bermondsey, for instance, are presently increasing at a rate second only to Kensington."

"And how does Dockside fit into this architectural renaissance?" Powell prompted dryly.

Atherton smiled. "I do get carried away, don't I? Dockside is a rather modest development in the scheme of things—forty-four one- and two-bedroom flats in a converted warehouse on the Thames in Rotherhithe, with an adjacent shopping and recreation complex across the road. We're rather proud of it, actually."

"I understand that part of the development is proposed on property presently owned by the borough . . ."

Atherton sighed. "Therein, Chief Superintendent, lies the root of the controversy you alluded to. We have an option to purchase the warehouse from its owners, but as you say, the council owns the land across the road. As you can imagine, it's difficult enough to put together a project of this nature without that sort of complication. Unfortunately, the commercial component is necessary to create a viable project, so we have made what we believe is a reasonable proposal to the council to purchase the property at the going rate. We're still waiting for a decision."

"I'm trying to put this as tactfully as possible, Mr. Atherton, but isn't the main bone of contention the fact that you'd be turning a number of council tenants out of their homes?"

Atherton looked mildly surprised at the implication of Powell's question. "One has to break a few eggs to make an omelette, Chief Superintendent. We're essentially transforming a slum into a livable, world-class community. Please don't misunderstand me—I don't mean to sound callous—but the long-term economic benefits will far outweigh the negative impact on a few individuals."

"I don't suppose they would see it that way," Powell observed.

"Richard Brighton understood the balance, and he was hardly what you would call a free-market fanatic," Atherton countered.

"How would you say that Brighton's death has affected Dockside's prospects?" Powell asked casually.

Atherton's brow furrowed. "As I say, I'm still waiting for planning approval from the council. Up until this point, they've been split about fifty-fifty. Richard was a strong advocate for the project. With him gone, there's a bit of a vacuum, I'm afraid." He left the rest unsaid.

Powell met his gaze. "Mr. Atherton, is it possible that someone could be so opposed to your project, they might employ desperate measures to stop it—murder, for instance?"

Atherton hesitated. "Anything's possible, I suppose. But as I said before, I simply can't believe that there could be any connection with what happened to Richard. We are, after all, dealing with what is essentially a political issue, and in this country we don't normally go around murdering our politicians."

"Point taken, Mr. Atherton. But I'd ask you to give the matter some further thought and get back to me if anything occurs to you." He handed over his card.

Atherton nodded. "Fair enough, Chief Superintendent."

Powell hesitated as he considered the best way to broach a potentially delicate subject. "There is the matter of Clive Morton to consider," he said offhandedly.

Atherton looked startled. "What do you mean?"

"I understand that Mr. Morton had an interest in Dockside."

"We had an arrangement whereby he would own and operate a restaurant on the quay. Something smart to give the place some ambience."

Powell scrutinized Atherton closely. "Clive Morton was murdered in a most unpleasant fashion earlier this week—the second person with a connection to Dockside to die in just over a month. I don't wish to alarm you, Mr. Atherton, but you'll have to admit it is a some-what remarkable occurrence of events."

"What are you suggesting, Chief Superintendent, that I might be next?"

"I'm not suggesting anything. At this point, there is no hard evidence connecting the two murders. I just wanted you to be aware of the possibility."

Atherton smiled grimly. "I wouldn't be completely honest with you if I tried to tell you that the thought hadn't occurred to me. However, Clive Morton was a person with large appetites, larger than life you might say. He had money, liked the wrong sort of girls, and was rumored to be a user of various, er, stimulants. I hesitate to speak ill of the dead, but it would be an under-statement to say that he tended to rub people the wrong way. I only knew him as a business associate, but my guess is he ran afoul of some supplier or pimp and un-fortunately paid the price."

"You're probably right," Powell rose to his feet. "Thank you, Mr. Atherton. You've been most helpful. Please don't hesitate to call me if you think of anything else."

Atherton looked thoughtful. "Of course."

It occurred to Powell as he stepped into Shad Thames that not once during Paul Atherton's discourse on the socioeconomic benefits of Dockside did he mention the millions of pounds that he personally stood to make from the scheme.

CHAPTER 12

Powell awoke on Saturday morning to a transparent blue sky full of birdsong and a garden full of trifidlike plants. He wasted no time in fleeing Surbiton, having made arrangements the previous evening to meet Tony Osborne at his flat in Soho first thing in the morning. After bolting down a bowl of something that tasted like little squares of cardboard, he drove in his Triumph TR4 to the train station and hurriedly secured the tonneau cover in the station car park. He only just managed to hop aboard the 9:54 to London Waterloo as it was about to pull away. The coach was packed with young couples off to London for a day's shopping, each it seemed with a statistically improbable clutch of three or four small children, which made for a diverting if mercifully short journey.

At Waterloo Station, he boarded the tube for Piccadilly amidst a crush of other travelers. Arriving at the last vacant seat in the coach at the same time as an elderly woman laden with shopping bags, he smiled and gestured for her to sit down.

She smiled wearily "Thanks, love," she said. "Me old dogs is killing me."

Powell held on as the coach hurtled through the darkness deep beneath the teeming streets of the city. The tube was not unlike a cosmologist's wormhole, he supposed fancifully. Disappear into a black hole and pop up, as if by magic, somewhere else in space and time—or at least at Embankment Station, he thought as the train slowed to a stop. *Mind the gap,* came the familiar admonishment over the loudspeaker.

He took a seat in the brief interval before the passengers getting on could fill the vacuum created by those leaving. As the train started up again, heads bobbed and swayed in unison with the rocking, lurching motion of the coach. A man intently perusing his *Racing Post*, another in a business suit with his eyes closed, and a young woman reading the *Sunday Times Style Magazine*, the tinny sound of an electronic drumbeat leaking from her earphones. No idle chatter here, just people immersed in their own affairs, quintessentially English and oddly comforting amidst these tatty surroundings. Powell felt a fond attachment to the aging, clanking Underground that was as much pragmatic as sentimental, since the alternative—driving anywhere in central London—was not a practical proposition.

In a long, windowless room in the middle of Scotland Yard known as the Central Command Complex, a team of officers monitor video images from three hundred cam-

eras fixed to lampposts and tall buildings throughout the
city, enabling them to skip, at the touch of a keypad, unen-
cumbered above the fray from Paddington to Piccadilly
to Pimlico, assessing traffic flow and congestion. Various
set computerized plans that control the sequence of traffic
signals are implemented, depending on the circumstances, to try and keep things moving. They don't like to
use the American term *gridlock*—which implies an or-
derly grid system of roads that does not exist in London,
where everything leads to the center—preferring instead
a system of color codes, ranging from green (traffic
moving freely) to black (bus driver with feet up reading
newspaper). The reality is the average speed of London
traffic is about ten miles an hour with vehicles spending a
third of their time stationary.

Powell's reverie was interrupted by a subdued chuckle
from the lady sitting next to him, who was engrossed in
a dog-eared paperback. He tried to read the title at the
top of the page nearest him without being too obvious
about it. *Malice in the Something-or-other.* He couldn't
make it out. A crime novel, probably. He wondered how
people could read such tripe. If real policemen operated the same way as fictional detectives, we'd all be in
big trouble, he thought, feeling superior—

"Ahem." It was the merest suggestion of a sound.

He looked up. A tall, middle-aged woman in a leather
coat was standing over him, staring at him, or rather
through him at his seat, no doubt imagining herself ensconced in it. He smiled benignly then looked away. It
was probable from an actuarial point of view that, being

a woman, she would live longer than he would anyway, so she could hardly begrudge him this small comfort for a few moments longer. Seconds later the train pulled into Piccadilly Circus Station.

Powell walked along Shaftesbury Avenue then turned up Great Windmill Street into the heart of Soho, the longtime haunt of immigrants, prostitutes, and bohos. He had wasted a good part of his youth prowling the narrow streets and alleys of London's unofficial red-light district looking for adventure, and although he tended to view life rather differently now, he still found Soho's cosmopolitan and raffish air stimulating. There is nowhere else in London where one can find such a juxtaposition of clubs, peep shows, clip joints, foreign restaurants, delicatessens, gay bars, market stalls, and media production houses—where prostitutes and junkies rub shoulders with businessmen, theatergoers, and politicians. Louche and slightly sinister, Soho was perhaps a little blander and more sanitized than it used to be, but it still wasn't a place to wander around alone at two in the morning.

He crossed Brewer Street into Lexington Street where Tony Osborne lived in a basement flat in a late-eighteenth-century terraced Georgian house. He descended the steps and knocked on the door, surprised to see the colorful flower boxes under the curtained windows on either side. The door opened to reveal a bleary-eyed Osborne dressed in wrinkled khakis and a white T-shirt.

"Morning, Tony," Powell said cheerily. "I hope I'm not too early."

Osborne scowled. "Don't just stand there, mate," he said. "Come in."

The flat consisted of a small sitting room with an adjoining kitchen and dining area and a bedroom in the back. The furniture was Swedish and functional, and the walls were decorated with abstract prints. The place was surprisingly neat and tidy.

"Have a seat," Osborne growled. "I'll get us some coffee."

"Thanks."

"Instant all right?" he called from the kitchen.

Powell grimaced. "Lovely."

Osborne returned presently with two mugs and a tin of sweetened milk. He sat down, added half the milk to his mug, then took a prodigious gulp. "Just what the doctor ordered," he said. "Now, then, first things first. My plane leaves at noon tomorrow." He reached into his trouser pocket. "Here's the key."

"Thanks again, Tony. I'm rather looking forward to a change of scene."

"Just don't wreck the place. It cost me an arm and a leg." He paused to drain his mug. "By the way, I checked with the Missing Persons Bureau, and no dead bodies matching Jill Burroughs's description have turned up in the past week."

"No news is good news, I suppose," Powell said soberly.

Osborne shrugged. "You know as well as I do that

people go missing all the time because of domestic arguments. She'll turn up eventually."

"I expect you're right. Still, it's been nearly a week."

"Look, mate, just to put your mind at ease, why not put out a news bulletin? She may not even realize that people are concerned about her." He looked at Powell. "Given the current state of your relations with the AC, it might be best if I put in the request."

Powell nodded. If Merriman ever found out that it was *he* who had made an inquiry at the Missing Persons Bureau about Jill Burroughs, the Assistant Commissioner would have his head impaled on a pike and prominently displayed atop the famous revolving sign in front of New Scotland Yard.

"Which raises a related point," Osborne continued. "I've written a memo to Merriman requesting your involvement in the Morton investigation because of a possible link with the Brighton murder." He grinned slyly. "I've couched it in terms of reducing duplication, better coordinating area and centralized functions, and more efficiently utilizing scarce financial and human resources. The little prig will have no choice but to agree, but it will no doubt piss him off severely."

Powell laughed. "I don't know what I'd do without you, Tony."

Osborne grunted. "Anything new on Morton?"

Powell summarized his conversations with Morton's housekeeper and Paul Atherton. "It seems our Clive was quite a lad. If he was in fact involved with prostitutes and drugs, there may not be much of a mystery about what happened to him, except for the details."

Osborne thought about this for a moment. "There's a bloke you might want to talk to. Les Wilkes. Small-time villain, basically harmless, knows just about everything that goes on in Soho in the vice line. We've used him as an informant from time to time. I'll leave you his address and phone number . . . Oh, yeah, before I forget, your rhymer, Simon Snavely? He's got a police record: intent to supply cocaine."

"Did your lads get round to searching his flat?"

Osborne nodded. "Clean as a whistle. You must have put the fear of God into him."

"Thanks, Tony. I owe you."

"Just make sure you water my bloody flowers, mate."

Powell stopped in at the Fitzrovia for lunch and learned from Celia Cross that there was still no word from Jill. Over his ploughman's he mentally organized his priorities for the following week. He needed to get on with interviewing Richard Brighton's colleagues on Southwark Council, Charles Mansfield and Adrian Turner—political rivals of Brighton, but for different reasons—as well as Tess Morgan, the community activist who represented the council tenants opposed to Dockside. He decided it would be best to back off on the Morton investigation until he got the official word from Merriman. It was an encounter he was beginning to look forward to. And he must remember to ring Marion in Canada to let her know about his new domestic arrangements. *Yes, love, I'll be staying at Tony Osborne's bachelor pad in Soho for a while—you know, the one I told you about with the black silk sheets on the bed.*

Don't worry, the garden will be just fine. No problem, Bob's your uncle, he thought fatalistically as he walked up to the bar to get another pint.

CHAPTER 13

Powell arrived at work on Monday in an uncharacteristically buoyant mood. A pleasant walk to Piccadilly Circus from Tony Osborne's flat, a short hop on the tube, with a change at Embankment for St. James's Park, and here he was strolling across Broadway on this fine spring morning. Through the glass doors into the main reception area of Scotland Yard—referred to for some arcane reason as the Back Hall—flashing a smile at the pretty constable on duty as he swiped himself in. He nearly collided with Merriman as he stepped out of the elevator. Into each life a little rain must fall.

"I want to see you in my office in five minutes," Sir Henry snarled.

"Yes, sir," Powell said in his most insufferably pleasant manner.

The Assistant Commissioner stormed off, and Powell proceeded to his office whistling tunelessly. He had a short conversation with Detective-Sergeant Black and then made some phone calls. He walked into Merriman's office a few minutes late.

The AC glared at him. "What do you think you're playing at, Powell?"

"Sir?"

"I've had a request from Osborne at West End Central. He wants you to take on the Morton file. What the hell is this all about?"

"Sorry I haven't kept you in the loop, sir, but Superintendent Osborne feels there could be a connection between Clive Morton and the Brighton case, which as you know I've been—"

"Don't tell me something I already know!" Merriman exploded. Then he sat in silence glaring at Powell, who could almost hear the wheels turning. Eventually, he turned his attention to some papers on his desk. "I want you to assign the file to Detective-Sergeant Evans," he said dismissively, signing something off with a flourish. "We need more women in the force with experience investigating serious crimes. As I have no doubt that both she and Black are capable of carrying out their duties with minimal supervision, this arrangement will enable you to assist me with a comprehensive planning report I'm preparing for the Commissioner." He looked up with a chilling smile. "I call it 'A Strategic Vision of Humane, Inclusive, and Flexible Policing for the Twenty-first Century.' And, oh, yes, Powell, don't mention anything to the press about a possible link between the two murders. We wouldn't want to start a panic, would we?"

* * *

The meeting in Powell's office later that morning with Detective-Sergeants Black and Evans was awkward for all of them. Evans's elation at being assigned to a murder investigation was tempered somewhat by the circumstances: Black was miffed at having to share the glory with Evans, and Powell, for his part, was furious.

When he had calmed down sufficiently, he tried to set the right tone with a positive note. "The main thing is we now have additional resources to work with—that means you, Evans. And, just to be clear, we will work together as a team; you may think of me, if you like, as your captain. I suggest we convene first thing each morning to compare notes and plan our next steps so we're not tripping all over one another. Are there any questions?"

"What about Merriman's report, sir?" Evans asked, concern sounding in her voice. "Won't he be expecting you to—"

"Merriman can shove his report up his arse," Powell replied brusquely, belying the inner turmoil he was experiencing. Recalling his Cambridge rock-climbing days, he felt like he was soloing an Exceptionally Severe without a rope.

Charles Mansfield's office was located in the ghastly London Bridge City complex that had risen in the last few years like an eruption of boils on the south bank of the Thames between the London and Tower Bridges. Mansfield, in his bespoke pinstriped suit, looked to be in his mid-thirties—surprisingly young for a Conservative these days—with wispy blond hair and pudgy features.

"Do make yourself comfortable, Chief Superintendent," he intoned ponderously. "Can I get you a drink—sherry, perhaps?"

"No, thank you."

They sat at a polished round table, placed a strategic distance from Mansfield's desk and intended to create an impression of relaxed collegiality but implying just the opposite.

"I understand you're a Cantabrigian, Chief Superintendent," Mansfield began smoothly.

Powell looked surprised.

The solicitor smiled. "I have my sources. I'm an Oxford man, myself. Nevertheless, it's heartening to see that the Metropolitan Police Service is in good hands."

"I think it would be accurate to say that the old-boy network is intact at the Yard," Powell responded coolly.

Mansfield seemed momentarily nonplussed, as if he was unsure how to interpret Powell's remark. "Yes, well, how exactly can I assist you, Chief Superintendent?"

"I'm looking for some background information on Richard Brighton. I was hoping you could help."

Mansfield looked amused. "We were hardly what you'd call the best of chums."

"I suppose rivals would be a better word," Powell suggested.

"*Political* rivals, yes. As you might expect, we didn't agree on many issues that came before council."

"Really? What about the proposed Dockside development in Rotherhithe?"

An almost imperceptible hesitation, then, "What about it?"

"I understand that both you and Brighton support it."

"I still do, but I'm not so sure about Richard—perhaps you could ring the Inferno and find out."

Powell regarded him impassively but said nothing.

Mansfield smiled easily. "I'm sorry, Chief Superintendent. That remark was in poor taste. It is true that we did agree on Dockside, but for fundamentally different reasons. Mine were born of principle, Richard's of expediency."

"Would you care to explain what you mean?"

"It is quite simple really. The Conservative Party believes in economic growth to create wealth and employment, thereby reducing the tax burden of the state on individuals and the social burden of individuals on the state. The Labour Party, on the other hand, has always stood for big government and big unions, both of which poison the well of the free market, leaving the rest of us to pay for their inept attempts at social engineering." His face contorted into a sneer. "*New* Labour, so-called, is no different—it's the nanny state in sheep's clothing, if I may coin a phrase. But, unfortunately, they've managed to deceive the entire bloody country." It was obviously a subject that was near and dear to his heart.

Powell sighed heavily. "I didn't ask for a speech, Mr. Mansfield. I simply want to know why you think Richard Brighton would lend his support to a project that, on the surface of it at least, conflicted with his political ideology."

A bitter laugh. "Richard's only ideology was opportunism. There was nothing he wouldn't do to further his own political interests."

"I should have thought that in this case, at least, he would have been concerned with the welfare of the hundred or so council tenants who are facing eviction from their homes."

Mansfield looked indignant. "What are you insinuating? That the Conservative Party is unmoved by the plight of these people?" He shook his head condescendingly. "It is so easy to take a simplistic approach to complex problems."

Powell's patience was stretching thin. "You still haven't answered my question," he said.

"Very well, Chief Superintendent. I'll make it easy for you to understand. Richard Brighton supported Dockside because he thought it would win him votes. End of story."

"Forgive me, but I thought that's what politics were all about."

"Political ambition is a noble impulse when it is informed by principle, Chief Superintendent."

"And what principle is that? Survival of the fittest?"

Mansfield's eyes narrowed. "I would very much appreciate it if you could get to the point, Chief Superintendent."

"I understand that Brighton was favored to be the next mayor of Southwark," Powell observed offhandedly.

"He made no secret of his desire in that respect," Mansfield replied frostily.

"I've also heard it said that you were considered to be his chief rival for the job."

"I have yet to declare my interest in the position." His tone was guarded now.

"I would imagine that with Brighton out of the picture, you'd have a clear field."

Mansfield affected a solemn demeanor. "I've learned in this business that *there is many a slip 'twixt the cup and the lip*, Chief Superintendent. However, if I *were* to be selected by my colleagues, I believe I could make a contribution to the borough."

Pompous little twit, Powell thought. He consulted his watch. "Is that the time? I won't keep you any longer, Mr. Mansfield, but I may need to talk to you again."

Mansfield smiled, except for his eyes. "The pleasure will be entirely mine, Chief Superintendent, I assure you."

Powell turned as he was going out the door. "Just one more question . . . The vote on Dockside—how do you think it will turn out in the end?"

"I have little doubt the project will eventually receive planning approval."

As Powell stepped into the sunlight, he could not dispel the curious notion that Mansfield had not sounded particularly enthusiastic about the prospect.

CHAPTER 14

The proposed Dockside development site was located on the Thames in Rotherhithe, midway between Tower Bridge and Limehouse Reach, where the river loops south to enclose the Isle of Dogs and Canary Wharf. As she drove east along Rotherhithe Street, Detective-Sergeant Evans, being something of a history buff, recalled the area's storied past. Rotherhithe, the thumb of marshy land jutting out into the Thames east of Bermondsey, had been a shipbuilding center long before the development of the Surrey Commercial Docks in the nineteenth century. Home of Edward III's palace, this is where his son the Black Prince fitted out his fleet, where the Mayflower set sail for America, and where Gulliver was born. The docks, which specialized in lumber trade with Scandinavia, burned for weeks during the Blitz and fell into gradual decline after the war.

Nowadays, the area was being transformed by property developers. Upscale warehouse conversions facing the river now existed cheek by jowl with decaying housing estates facing inward, emphasizing the gulf between rich and poor, home owner and tenant. Crime was rampant on the council estates—burglaries, racial offenses, and petty crimes committed mostly by young people—representing a serious social problem. Bored kids with little to do and even fewer prospects. Sarah Evans had been born and bred in the East End, raised by a single mother, and was no stranger to the stresses imposed by poverty and peer pressure. While she could not countenance using deprivation as an excuse for antisocial behavior, she could sympathize with the anger and frustration experienced by people like Tess Morgan who were leading the charge to oppose the Dockside development. Such were Evans's thoughts as she turned into the Southwark Park Council Estate.

The council estate consisted of two squat concrete blocks of flats with a weed-infested playground on one side and a car park on the other. Across Rotherhithe Street, fronting the river, was a derelict brick warehouse. Tess Morgan lived in the block closest to the road on the ground floor.

The door of Number 11 opened to reveal a slight woman in her early forties with long, curly red hair.

Detective-Sergeant Evans introduced herself. "I hope I'm not late," she said. "The traffic on Tower Bridge was unbelievable."

Tess Morgan smiled sympathetically. "I know what you mean. I can't wait for the new tube station to open at Jamaica Road. Assuming we're still here, that is," she added on a somber note. "Look, why don't we go for a walk—I've been cooped up all day."

Evans smiled. "Fine."

"I'll just leave a note for my daughter in case she gets home from school before we get back. I'd ask you in for a cup of tea, but things look rather a fright at the moment. Monday's my day off—I work at a bookstore in the village—but I seem to spend all my spare time these days writing letters." She looked apologetic.

"Shall I meet you outside then?" Evans asked.

Tess Morgan brushed a wisp of hair from her face. "Give me a few minutes."

Detective-Sergeant Evans sat on a bench in the deserted playground beside a rusting jungle gym, pondering a seesaw that looked oddly askew. A few moments later, Tess Morgan appeared.

"It's a lovely day," she said. "Why don't we go for a walk along the river?"

They crossed the road and walked south along a chain-link fence behind the derelict Dockside warehouse until they came to a new apartment complex consisting of two converted warehouse buildings with a cobbled walkway between them providing access to the river.

"This is what Cool Britannia is all about," Tess remarked bitterly as they walked out onto the quay. "Three hundred thousand pounds for a one-bedroom flat. While the rest of us struggle to put food on the table for our families."

Evans looked up at the smart brick buildings with their blue balconies. "I've often wondered who can afford to pay those prices."

"There's no shortage of people queuing up for the opportunity, I can tell you that. Don't get me wrong, I've no problem with having a mix of luxury and affordable housing in the community. I wouldn't even object to Dockside if it was confined to the old warehouse site." Her eyes flashed angrily. "But I'll be damned if I'm going to sit back and let a profit-mad developer and his friends on council put ordinary people out of their homes. There's nothing wrong with our flats that a lick of paint won't put right."

Evans frowned. "What about the council? Surely they must have the interests of the community at heart?"

Tess looked at her. "You're joking. It all comes down to money. The value of property along the Thames has soared, and the council only sees pound signs. Of course they argue that selling off the more valuable estates will raise money to improve social housing elsewhere in the borough. But the bottom line is they don't want ordinary people living here anymore. Gentrification is the euphemism for what's happening in this community, but it's really a kind of social cleansing."

Evans could think of nothing to say as they walked along the quay, the Thames sparkling in the sunlight and off to the right in the distance the gleaming glass tower of Canary Wharf. Soon they stood in front of the old warehouse, which was situated on a piece of derelict ground between the block of flats with the blue balconies and another new development with a terra-cotta facade farther along the quay.

"Well, this is it," Tess pronounced. "Doesn't look like much now, does it?"

The five-story warehouse, with its crumbling masonry, rusting ironwork, and blank, staring windows, had obviously seen better days. In black letters on the front face at the top of the building, and just barely legible, was painted DOCKSIDE SHIPPING CO.

"What exactly is the proposal here, Ms. Morgan?"

"Forty one- and two-bedroom flats, four penthouse apartments, and a restaurant below. Like I said before, I don't have a particular problem with that part. However, the developer maintains that, based on his costs, the project is only economic if it's linked to a new commercial development—shops and so forth—across the road on the council estate. This would entail demolishing one of the blocks—the one I live in, as a matter of fact. He's offered to leave the other building standing as a sop to the council, a sort of token monument to enlightened social planning. But before he can proceed any further, the council has to agree to sell or let him a portion of the property. I get the impression he's in a rather dodgy financial position. He's got some sort of option to purchase the warehouse building that has to be renewed periodically. The longer it takes to get planning approval, the more money it costs him—"

"I take it that's where you come in," Evans interjected.

Tess's face tightened. "You're bloody right. The developer's problem becomes an opportunity for us. We're prepared to do whatever it takes to delay the project, to stop it altogether if we can. Even if I wasn't personally affected, I'd feel the same way. I'm not interested in living in a city that treats its citizens like chattel."

"I'm still a bit puzzled about something," Evans said. "I should have thought there'd be considerable pressure on your local councillor to take a strong stand against the project."

Tess frowned. "That one's as useless as tits on a bull. Oh, he'll vote against it if he wants to get reelected, but so far he's distinguished himself by avoiding the debate entirely. Doesn't want to be accused of taking the 'narrow view,' if you can believe it!"

"What about Richard Brighton?" Evans asked casually.

Tess tossed her a curious look. "What about him?"

"I understand he was a big supporter of Dockside."

"He could afford to be, couldn't he? It wasn't in his ward; it didn't affect the voters who elected him, so he could claim the high ground by appearing to have his eye on the interests of the majority. Besides, Brighton was bound for bigger and better things, mayor of Southwark, then mayor of London, possibly. Maybe even bloody prime minister someday. To get on in politics these days you have to kowtow to the City."

"Did you ever discuss it with him directly?"

"We met a number of times."

"How did he respond to your concerns?"

Tess thought about this for a moment. "I think he was sympathetic at some level, but it was essentially a political issue for him: choosing the course of action that was in the best interests of Richard Brighton and the Labour Party."

"The thing is, Ms. Morgan, he ended up dead, murdered in cold blood. And I'm wondering if it could possibly have something to do with Dockside."

She looked at Evans with an odd expression on her face. "What are you suggesting?"

"Nothing at all," Evans replied quickly. "I'm just trying to determine if there could be a connection."

"I'm afraid I can't help you," she said in a flat voice. She checked her watch. "I really should be getting back. I always like to be there when Rachel gets home from school."

"What will happen to you?" Evans asked. "I mean, if Dockside goes ahead?"

She shrugged. "I don't like to think about it. Rachel's at a decent school now and seems to be settling down. But we'll have to move, I suppose, if we can find a decent place somewhere we can afford."

Evans smiled empathetically. "You'd better go meet your daughter. I can find my way back to my car. And Ms. Morgan . . ."

"Yes?"

"Good luck."

The woman smiled wanly. "Thanks."

When she was alone, Detective-Sergeant Evans leaned over the quayside railing and gazed into the murky waters of the Thames.

CHAPTER 15

As was his practice, Detective-Sergeant Bill Black stopped in at his local on the way home from work. He selected a table near the window well away from the rest and took a grateful sip of beer. He wiped the foam from his upper lip and then, as was also his practice when he was involved in a challenging case, he proceeded to lay his mental cards on the table—a sort of deductive solitaire, as he liked to think of it. It was a way for him to put his thoughts in order and sort things through in an organized manner.

Black had long ago recognized his limitations and suspected that there were some who thought him plodding and uncreative. And while he realized that he was unlikely to ever rise above his present rank in the force, he was content with the knowledge that he was good at his job and commanded the respect of his peers at the Yard. Too many times he had seen a colleague promoted only to be beaten down by the bureaucracy. He often wondered how Mr. Powell, whom he considered practical (the highest compliment that can be paid by a policeman to his superior), managed to maintain his sanity. Although he found him moody and abrasive at times, Black had a great deal of respect for his mercurial superior and believed that his super felt the same way about him.

He was also proud of the fact that he had always made an effort to better himself. Not having the benefit of a university education, which you really needed these days to get on in the Met, he had enrolled in evening classes at his local college to broaden his horizons and to keep his mind sharp. Last year, he had immersed himself in Adventures in English Literature; this year, he was considering Philosophy Through the Ages, if he could fit it in with the cabinetry course that Muriel wanted him to take. The thing is you had to play the hand you were dealt in life. The cards might be fixed, but how you played them was up to you.

A thought that brought his attention back to the problem at hand: Was there a link between the murders of Richard Brighton and Clive Morton? The fact that Morton had planned to open a restaurant at Dockside, the controversial development scheme that Richard Brighton had been so vocal in supporting, was a striking coincidence, to say the least. He mentally turned over another card: Clive Morton's involvement with drugs and prostitutes and the gruesome manner in which he had died. If Morton had in fact been done by a ponce or a pusher and Brighton by a blagger, that was the end of the story. All nice and tidy. Except he couldn't get his mind off all those council tenants who would be displaced by the Dockside development. Even more worrisome, he had been thinking a lot lately about Mr. Powell's young friend—the missing Canadian girl, Jill Burroughs, and her secret admirer, Simon Snavely, the drug pusher. And the fact that the young lady had been bothered in the pub by Clive Morton the same night that Snavely had tried to follow her home, and just two nights before Morton was murdered. Realizing with characteristic self-awareness that he wasn't going to win this particular game, Black packed up his mental cards and went up to the bar to get another pint.

The next morning, Powell met Adrian Turner, the Labour councillor, at a small cafe in Tooley Street, Southwark. Turner was a humorless young man with a chip on his shoulder who appeared to take himself very seriously. Incongruously, he reminded Powell of a younger Merriman.

"Why did you want to see me?" he asked directly.

"I won't mince words, Mr. Turner. I'm trying to find out who murdered Richard Brighton."

"Your time would be better spent, in my opinion, rooting out corruption in the Metropolitan Police Service."

Powell mentally sighed. He could tell that it was going to be one of those days. "On the night of March eleventh, Richard Brighton was murdered not far from here. I was wondering if you might be able to shed some light on the matter." He left it open-ended.

A suspicious look crossed Turner's face. "What's this all about anyway? I thought he was mugged."

"I wouldn't be doing my job if I didn't consider every possibility."

Turner laughed hollowly. "Your bloody job. That's rich. Keeping the working class in its place is the job of the police."

"Spare me the agitprop. You seem to have lost sight of the fact that a man's been murdered."

"On the contrary, I think about it every day."

"What exactly do you think about, Mr. Turner?"

"Karma, Chief Superintendent. Or the wages of sin, if you prefer."

A theologian, no less. "Are you suggesting that Brighton got what he deserved?" Powell asked mildly.

"That would be rather presumptuous of me, I think."

"Perhaps you could clear something up for me. You're a member of the Labour Party, as was Richard Brighton, yet I get the distinct impression you didn't see eye to eye. Correct me if I'm wrong, but I can only assume that you represent some sort of fringe group within the party."

"What the hell are you talking about?"

Powell shrugged. "It's obvious, isn't it? Richard Brighton was clearly the standard-bearer for the Labour Party in Southwark. By all accounts, he would have been the next mayor if somebody hadn't killed him. And the eventual success of the Dockside project will be due in no small part to his efforts in support of it."

Turner looked at him without expression. "You're trying to provoke me, aren't you? Well, it won't work. Because you're dead wrong about Dockside. It will never happen. People around here are finally waking up to the corporate agenda. There's no question that Richard's misguided support gave the project a boost at the start, but the tide was beginning to turn. I think even he recognized that. Ironically, his death has probably increased support for Dockside—a temporary manifestation of public sympathy no doubt—but that will soon pass. So you see, Chief Superintendent, it was Richard who was becoming marginalized, not me."

"Surely it's not all black and white, Mr. Turner."

"It bloody well *is* black and white!" Turner rejoined, showing the first sign of emotion. "Dockside is the architectural embodiment of Thatcherism. It's smash-and-grab development of the worst kind. Where are the basic amenities, the green spaces, the public areas? Why was there no consultation with the local community? I'll tell you why. Because we no longer live in a democratic society. Because all those tenants facing eviction have no bloody rights. It's that simple. Let me give you a little history lesson, Chief Superintendent. The London Docklands Development Corporation was set up in 1981 to preside, supposedly, over the rejuvenation of the London docks. In reality, the LDDC was an undemocratic body imposed on us by Mrs. Thatcher to feather the nests of her friends in the City. One hundred percent tax relief on capital expenditures, no business rates for ten years, and freedom from planning controls were some of the tactics used. The LDDC was quite rightly opposed by the Greater London Council, and you know what happen to the GLC. She simply abolished it. The LDDC finished its work in 1998, and we are now living with the legacy: two cultures, rich and poor, unaffordable pleasure domes like Dockside amidst huge swaths of dereliction, gleaming office towers rising above the ghettos. I don't know about you, but it's not the kind of community I want my children to live in."

Powell had to admit that he had some empathy for Adrian Turner's polarized view of the world. After all, good and evil, right and wrong, guilt and innocence were the stock and trade of the law as well. However, look at a monochrome photograph of anyone and you will see more shades of gray than black or white. The battered wife who lashes out at her tormentor with a bread knife; the addict who breaks into someone's home to support his habit; the motorist, in a momentary lapse of attention, who strikes and kills a small child. But while we are all of us imperfect and fallible, we must ultimately be held accountable as individuals for our actions. Powell held this precept alone as an absolute truth in a relativistic universe.

"One more question, Mr. Turner: If everything you say is true, why do you suppose Richard Brighton supported Dockside?"

Turner smiled, but it looked more like a sneer. "I'll let you be the judge of that, Chief Superintendent."

CHAPTER 16

When Powell got back to the Yard, there was a message from Sir Reginald Quick, the Senior Home Office Pathologist, waiting for him. He rang back but got the engaged signal. He swore silently. He was debating whether he should pay a visit on spec to the Forensic Science Service Metropolitan Laboratory in Lambeth Road, where Sir Reggie presided in splendid isolation, when Detective-Sergeant Evans walked into his office.

"Well, Evans?" he asked.

She proceeded to fill him in on yesterday's conversation with Tess Morgan. "She's a woman on a mission, there's no question about that. And who can blame her? Besides the prospect of losing her home, she's got a teenage daughter to worry about. Frankly, I don't know how she does it: raising her kid, holding down a full-time job, leading the campaign against Dockside."

"A woman's work is never done," Powell remarked dangerously.

Evans glared at him.

"Would you consider yourself a political animal by nature, Evans?"

She looked surprised by this question. "What do you mean?"

"Are you a card-carrying member of a political party? A true believer in the dogma of either the right or the left?"

"With all due respect, sir, that's between me and my cat."

Powell smiled. "You're quite right, of course. However, I will share *my* thoughts on the matter with you, fresh as they are from my recent encounters with two members of one of our local councils. I am going to let you in on a secret, Evans, the dirty little secret that lies at the heart of our democratic system. Politics as we know it is essentially a contest between conflicting versions of the truth; since by definition there can be only one truth, the entire system is based on a pack of lies. In the House of Commons, you can call a member a whore, a poltroon, or a drunk, but never a liar. Because that would expose the whole bloody farce for what it is."

He noticed the bemused expression on her face. "Why is this relevant, you ask? Because I've come to the conclusion that Charles Mansfield and Adrian Turner are both liars. They are each fanatics in their own right, and they hated Richard Brighton for what he was and what he stood for. The question is: Is there any more to it than that?"

"Is that a rhetorical question, sir?"

Before he could make an appropriate reply, Sergeant

Black lumbered into the office. He wore a solemn expression on his face.

"Excuse me, sir, but I just got a call from someone claiming to have the inside track on Dockside. He says he has evidence that Charles Mansfield, the local councillor, has a secret financial interest in the project, placing him in a conflict-of-interest position."

"What evidence?" Powell asked sharply.

"He didn't say, sir. He rang off before I could press him."

"Did you recognize the voice?"

"Sorry, sir."

Powell sat in silence trying to grasp the potential implications of this anonymous phone call. He looked at Evans. "I rest my case," he said.

Before confronting Charles Mansfield with what was, after all, an unsubstantiated allegation at this point, Powell decided that it might be wise to discreetly query Paul Atherton on the financial aspects of Dockside.

Atherton answered on the first ring.

"Mr. Atherton, Chief Superintendent Powell. Sorry to bother you again so soon, but I have a few more questions, I'm afraid."

"Fire away, Chief Superintendent."

"When we last spoke, you mentioned that you had an arrangement with Clive Morton whereby he would have owned and operated a restaurant at Dockside."

"Chez Clive, that's it."

"Did Morton have any other financial interest in the project?"

"He had a ten percent share in addition to the restaurant. He was a junior partner, in effect."

"Do you have any other partners?"

"No. Why do you ask?" He sounded genuinely curious.

"Force of habit, Mr. Atherton. Perhaps you could clear something else up for me. I understand that you don't own the warehouse property outright but have an option to purchase the property once you get planning approval. Is that how it works?"

A slight hesitation. "You've obviously been doing your homework, Chief Superintendent. Yes, that's how it works. The option is renewable every six months subject to an additional payment."

"So the longer it takes to get the council's blessing, the more your costs increase?"

"I'm afraid so. Just between you and me, I'll be in dire straits if I can't put this thing to bed by the end of the summer. As you can imagine, it would be difficult to raise additional money at that point because of the uncertainty surrounding the project. However, if and when I get the green light, I've got a commitment from my bank for the funds required to purchase the council property. Basically, it all hinges on the politicians now."

Not an enviable position to be in, Powell thought. "Thank you, Mr. Atherton. I appreciate your candor."

"Not at all, Chief Superintendent."

After he'd rung off, Powell wondered about the best way to approach Charles Mansfield. He had no reason not to believe Atherton, but the anonymous phone call had obviously been intended to cast a spotlight on Mansfield for some reason. If there had been some sort of understanding between Atherton and Mansfield, was it possible that Brighton had found out about it somehow and then threatened to expose them? It occurred to him that if there was a financial agreement of some kind, documents must exist somewhere. He made a mental note to have Evans look into it. His thoughts suddenly turned to Adrian Turner, the po-faced young socialist— perhaps the opposition was up to some dirty tricks. And what about Tess Morgan, the community activist? Even a hint of scandal at this point could well tip the balance of opinion against Dockside.

He picked up the phone and rang Charles Mansfield's office. Mansfield was in a meeting so he left a message with his secretary.

CHAPTER 17

Sir Reginald Quick's office at the Forensic Science Service Metropolitan Laboratory was located more or less at the center of the building. As Powell made his way through a labyrinth of antiseptic-smelling corridors that would have done Daedalus proud, he caught occasional glimpses of white-coated boffins bustling about in gleaming laboratories. He eventually arrived at Sir Reggie's lair and knocked on the door.

"Come!"

Sir Reggie's office was a cramped and cluttered room filled with file cabinets, books, stacks of reports, and various liquid-filled sample jars with mercifully unidentifiable objects suspended in them. The pathologist sat hunched over a desk that looked far too small for him, pecking with two fingers at a computer keyboard. "Don't hover, man. Sit down, for God's sake!"

"Er, where?"

"On the bloody chair, where else? Just move those papers."

Powell did as he was told.

Sir Reggie continued typing. "I'm just about finished with this damn thing," he muttered.

"Technical report?" Powell asked harmlessly.

Sir Reggie's large, florid face suddenly grew even redder. "The Hampstead Amateur Players, of which my wife is a leading light, are putting on *My Fair Lady* next month," he explained, "and I've been lumbered with doing the bloody program." He turned to look at Powell, his white hair askew and a dismal expression on his face. "Victoria is playing Eliza," he said.

Powell dared not crack a smile. He knew that Sir Reggie's spouse, Victoria, was a woman to be reckoned with, both in terms of physical presence and force of personality. But the thought of her playing the simple cockney flower girl beggared the imagination. "That's nice," he said lamely.

"Perhaps I could sell you a pair of tickets," the pathologist ventured slyly.

"Er, thanks all the same, Reggie, but my wife's away, and I don't get out much."

Sir Reggie sighed heavily. "All right, Powell, let's get on with it. What do you want?"

"Did you have a look at those postmortem reports I sent over? The Morton and Brighton files," Powell prompted.

Sir Reggie frowned. "They must be somewhere around here . . . I put them on your chair, I think. What the hell have you done with them?"

Powel smiled. "On the corner of your desk."

"Oh, right." He flipped quickly through the reports as

if to verify that he had in fact seen them before. He returned them to their pile and looked appraisingly at Powell. "Yes?"

"I was wondering if you could see any similarities in the two cases?"

He pondered this for a moment. "Now that you mention it . . . they're both bloody dead!" He laughed uproariously.

Powell dutifully smiled. "Besides that."

"Be precise, man!" Sir Reggie roared. "What sort of similarities?"

"Brighton drowned and Morton bled to death as a result of a knife wound. That much is clear. I'm more interested in the fact that they were both struck on the head with unknown blunt objects prior to death."

"Ah, yes," Sir Reggie snorted, "the convenient blunt object, the forensic equivalent of the proverbial black box!"

Powell looked puzzled.

"There is a deplorable absence of rigor in modern forensic practice despite all the ballyhoo you hear about DNA and other scientific marvels. If a villain farts at a crime scene, I expect it won't be long before we'll be able to test the air with some gadget that will identify the culprit ninety-nine times out of a hundred with an error of plus or minus three percent. But none of this wizardry is a substitute for experience and bloody hard work."

"I'm not sure I understand . . ."

"Don't get me wrong, the pathologists involved did

decent jobs—I know both of 'em personally—they just didn't take it to that next step. Of course, they don't have the benefit of reviewing the other's work, as I have," he added charitably.

Powell waited patiently for more. He had learned from hard experience that the best way to extract information from Sir Reggie was to appear disinterested. The Senior Home Office Pathologist had a reputation as a brilliant eccentric who had little patience with the intellectual deficiencies of lesser mortals. While his storied abilities seemed at times to have less to do with the scientific method than an uncanny sense of intuition, no one, in Powell's experience, could read the entrails of forensic mysteries like Sir Reggie. And to his further credit, he bore his title humbly, almost with embarrassment, refusing to be called Sir Reginald by anyone he was on remotely civil terms with.

"Taking the Brighton chap first," he continued, "the appearance of the body at postmortem clearly points to drowning as the cause of death. The external signs—the foam cap around the mouth and nostrils and the piece of flotsam found locked in his right hand as a result of cadaveric spasm—were corroborated by the appearance of the lungs as well as the presence of water in the stomach."

Powell knew all this already, having read the postmortem report himself, but he was content to let Reggie warm to his subject.

"The injury to the back of the head was relatively inconsequential in this case. The energy of the blow was

just sufficient to produce a distinctive depressed frac-
ture of the outer table of the skull, leaving the inner table
intact. It probably contributed to the victim's death only
in as much as it likely rendered him temporarily unconscious, or at least stunned him, before he ended up in the
river, thereby facilitating his eventual drowning."

"Getting back to the head wound—"

"All in good time," Sir Reggie said gruffly. "Now
then, turning to the case of Clive Morton—a great loss,
by the way," he added parenthetically. "I respect a chap
who refuses to be ripped off and isn't afraid to tell it like
it is."

Powell wasn't surprised.

"Morton died of exsanguination as a result of an in-
cised wound to the left side of the neck that severed the
jugular vein. The angle of the cut is consistent with a
right-handed assailant standing over the victim. Because we're dealing with a cut rather than a stab wound,
it is unfortunately not possible to ascertain much about
the nature of the edged weapon that was used in the attack. There were no defensive wounds, so one can assume the victim was unconscious at the time the coup de
grâce was administered."

"Lovely," Powell remarked. "Then he stuffs an apple
in poor old Clive's cake-hole."

"Obviously a hard-*core* villain. Ha ha!"

"Er, very good, Reggie, but if we might return to my
original question. You've provided an excellent summary
of how the two cases differ; I'm interested in finding out
if there are any similarities."

Sir Reggie leaned back in his chair at a precarious

angle and stared at the ceiling. "Context, Powell, I must have context if I am to devote any more mental energy to this problem."

Powell briefly summarized the case for a possible link between the two murders. "The fact they both were connected to the Dockside development is either one hell of a coincidence or else someone out there is *dead* set against the project going ahead," he concluded wryly.

Sir Reggie smiled grudgingly. "At first blush," he said, "the attacks would seem to be quite different in character. Bludgeoning is most commonly associated with unpremeditated attacks—an assault carried out in the heat of passion with the first heavy object that comes to hand. A mugging gone wrong is another plausible scenario that is consistent with the particulars of the Brighton case. The victim is accosted by a mugger, attempts to flee, and is struck on the back of the head. The villain panics and disposes of the evidence in the Thames. Clive Morton's murder, on the other hand, positively smacks of premeditation. It is true that the victim was struck on the back of the head in much the same manner as Brighton, except much harder. But it is the next step in the sequence of events that is suggestive. After knocking him unconscious, his assailant then takes the trouble to prop him up against a refuse bin before methodically slitting his throat—"

"Methodically?"

"One neat, deep cut as opposed to a number of clumsy attempts. Leaving aside the significant fact that he was found with his wallet still on him, which would seem to preclude robbery as a motive, there is the business of the apple to consider. It was obviously intended to make a point."

Powell frowned. "Yes, but what point?"

"You're the bloody detective," Sir Reggie rejoined.

"So you're saying the two crimes have little in common—"

"I didn't say that. I said at *first blush*."

"What do you mean?"

"I've carefully examined the photographs taken at postmortem and have made some measurements of the depressed fractures of the skull in each case. The indentations in both cases had three sides—that is, flat at the deepest point with the other two sides sloping outward. Based on the distinctive character and shape of the marks, I can only come to one conclusion . . ." He paused dramatically for effect. "Both injuries were inflicted by a heavy object, probably hexagonal in cross section, approximately an inch and a half in diameter. Although I can't be absolutely certain, it is likely, indeed probable, that the same weapon was used in both attacks."

Powell's mind whirled as the import of this revelation struck home. "What kind of weapon?" he asked mechanically.

The pathologist shrugged. "It's a bit of a poser."

CHAPTER 18

It was going on four o'clock when Powell finished up at the lab, so he was able to persuade himself that there was little point in returning to the office. On the way back to Tony's flat, he stopped at a pub in Berwick Street for a restorative. He spent the next hour smoking and mulling over the implications of Sir Reggie's findings. If in fact Richard Brighton and Clive Morton were murdered by the same person, which now seemed likely, then one had to wonder who might be next. It was possible, of course, that the crimes had been committed by different individuals using similar weapons. But the somewhat unusual shape of the object described by Sir Reggie made this scenario unlikely. The possibility of separate random attacks by the same person seemed even more remote. One could only assume, therefore, that the killings had something to do with Dockside, the only thing the two men were known to have in common at this point. Which raised the chilling possibility that there could well be others on the murderer's hit list. Paul

Atherton, the developer, for one. Perhaps the first two murders had been intended to scare him off. Powell frowned at his empty glass.

Then there was Charles Mansfield. Someone was evidently out to discredit him with the accusation that the he stood to benefit financially from Dockside. And with Brighton out of the picture, Mansfield had, by default, assumed the mantle of head cheerleader for the project on Southwark Council.

The question was, Who stood to gain the most from Dockside's demise? Tess Morgan leapt immediately to mind. Evans had seemed favorably impressed by the woman, but there was no denying that she had a lot to lose if the project went ahead, as did the hundred or so other tenants she represented.

After two pints and half a dozen cigarettes, Powell realized he was rapidly approaching the point of diminishing returns, so he left the pub, stopping in the street market to purchase an eggplant. He was pleasantly surprised to bump into Sarah Evans, who was poring over the kiwis at a fruit stall. "This is a surprise," he said.

She smiled. "I often stop here on the way home from work. You can find some incredible bargains at this time of day."

Powell contemplated the bleak prospect of another evening alone. "Look, Evans, if you don't have any plans, I mean if you're not busy, why don't you come back to my flat with me and I'll make us dinner . . ." He trailed off awkwardly.

She looked at him suspiciously. "Your flat?"

Powell explained about Tony Osborne.

"I see, a little home away from home, is that the idea, sir?"

"Something like that."

When Evans had worked with Powell previously on the Yorkshire moors murder case, she had felt herself attracted to him, as she sensed he was to her. He was, however, married, not to mention the fact that he was her superior. And she had her career to think about. By unspoken agreement, they had identified the boundary in their relationship over which neither of them was willing to step. She had the impression that Powell compensated for this by affecting a certain formality in his manner toward her at work. Being competitive by nature, she felt that he was always testing her in the most aggravating fashion. Curiously enough, they were much more relaxed in their social relationship—an arrangement with which they both seemed comfortable.

"Well, what do you say?" he was asking.

She smiled. "Why not? As long as you're doing a curry, that is."

Sarah Evans wandered around the flat with a glass of white wine as Powell got things ready in the kitchen. She emerged from the bedroom shaking her head in amazement. "Wow, black silk sheets!"

Powell smiled sheepishly. "What can I say?"

"Are you almost ready? I'm starving."

"Come over here and pay attention, Evans. I am going to show you how to prepare *brinjal bharta*. Right. I've already heated the oil in this pot. I'm adding a half teapoon of cumin seeds and a quarter teaspoon of black mustard seeds. Now I'll put the lid on until the mustard seeds start to pop."

Evans listened intently to the seeds sizzling in the oil. After about thirty seconds, she began to hear a faint pinging sound like miniature popcorn explosions.

"Now then," Powell said briskly, uncovering the pot. "I'm going to fry one chopped onion and one table-spoon each of finely chopped garlic and ginger until they're golden brown." The ingredients hit the hot oil with a loud *chum*. "While I'm doing this, I'd like you take that eggplant on the counter there, remove the skin, then mash it up in a bowl."

Evans regarded the large eggplant doubtfully. The skin was blackened and wrinkled as if it had been scorched with a blow torch.

"It's supposed to look that way, Evans. I previously roasted it over a flame—you could do it under a grill or on a barbecue—to give it a sort of smoky flavor. Now get to work and be careful—it's hot."

As she mashed away, Powell added two chopped green chilies to the pot for heat, a coarsely chopped tomato, and a half teaspoon of turmeric powder. "If you're too lazy to use the individual spices, this is the point you could add a good teaspoon of curry powder in place of the cumin, mustard, and turmeric. I'll stir fry this for five or ten minutes until the oil separates from the mixture and floats to the surface. Then I'll add the mashed eggplant, a tablespoon of lemon juice, and salt to taste, then cover and simmer for about fifteen minutes."

Evans, who rarely had time to cook for herself, shook

her head in admiration. "I'll never remember all this, you know."

Powell smiled. "Then you'll just have to keep coming over until you do. Time for another glass of wine before dinner, I think."

A half hour later, Powell presented Evans with the fragrant vegetable curry, garnished with cilantro and served with basmati rice and the *chapatis* they had picked up on the way home at the Indian takeaway around the corner.

After they had demolished the meal, Powell put the kettle on for the coffee press. "I get my beans from Starbucks," he said, thinking about Jill Burroughs.

Evans groaned contentedly. "You've missed your calling. You should quit the force and open a restaurant here in Soho, call it Powell's Palace of Pappadams or something like that."

He looked at her. "You're just after my job."

She laughed unselfconsciously. "Is it that obvious?"

Powell grinned, then said casually, "I went to see Sir Reggie this afternoon. I asked him to take a look at the Brighton and Morton postmortem reports."

She perked up. "Oh, yes?"

He told her about the pathologist's conclusion.

"It looks like we're finally on to something," she said, her eyes bright.

"Thank you for that insight, Evans."

"I mean, it's obvious, isn't it? Someone is determined to put a stop to Dockside and will stop at nothing to do it. If you want my opinion, I think he killed Richard Brighton in an act of desperation and then, when he realized he'd gotten away with it, he planned Clive Morton's murder—"

"You said *he*," Powell pointed out.

"Well, the way Morton was murdered—it's not the sort of thing a woman would do."

"Tell that to Mr. and Mrs. Borden."

Evans frowned. "You think Tess Morgan had something to do with it, don't you?"

He poured their coffees. "We can't rule anything out at this point. After all, we don't know much about her. Perhaps she has a boyfriend who is fanatically devoted to the cause, or maybe one of the other people she represents is more desperate than she is. Don't forget it was a man who called about Charles Mansfield. In any case, I think we need to look a little more closely at Ms. Morgan's disgruntled band of council tenants before we draw any firm conclusions." He took a sip of his coffee. "There is, of course, a more fundamental flaw in your reasoning."

She regarded him warily. "And what might that be?"

"Why kill Morton? He had a relatively small interest in the project. And the same question could be asked about Brighton. Why not just get rid of Atherton, the developer, and be done with it?"

"What are you driving at?"

Powell paused thoughtfully. "I think we need to find out if Clive Morton and Richard Brighton had something else in common besides Dockside."

After walking Evans to the tube station in Tottenham Court Road, Powell wandered back through the heart of

Soho, taking in the sights and sounds. The narrow, crowded streets, the smell of garlic, laughing people spilling out of restaurants on their way to the theater, faces crowded behind pub windows and kids sleeping rough in urine-stained doorways.

He found himself in Rupert Street, amidst the gaudy pink and blue neon signs proclaiming GIRLS GIRLS GIRLS, BOOKS VIDEOS MAGAZINES, and SCHOOLGIRL MODELS UP-STAIRS. A man in a camel-hair coat, who looked like a slightly sinister Phil Collins, stood with his hands in his pockets and a cigarette in his mouth at the entrance to a narrow alleyway. Behind him, partially hidden in a dimly lit doorway beneath a sign that said PEEP SHOW, Powell could see a blonde woman in a short skirt. He approached the man and smiled.

The man looked him up and down. "Good evening, mate. What's your fancy—videos or live entertainment?"

CHAPTER 19

The next morning in Powell's office, Detective-Sergeant Black was reporting on his further inquiries into Clive Morton's affairs. "It turns out that Morton did have a regular dining companion—just like you thought, sir—a model named Samantha Jones."

Evans shot Powell a withering glance.

He coughed politely. "This is most interesting, Black. Please continue."

"Yes, sir. Miss Jones went to great lengths to make it clear there was nothing romantic going on between them. They were just casual acquaintances, as she put it."

"That's consistent with what his housekeeper told me about Morton's love life. Tell me, Black, Ms. Jones wouldn't be the kind of model who advertises in call boxes, by any chance?"

Black grinned self-consciously. "No, sir. She looks more like your high-fashion type. And quite ambitious, I'd say. I get the impression that she went out with Morton just so she could be seen in fancy restaurants with a celebrity of sorts."

"What a girl's gotta do to get ahead," Evans rejoined.

Powell ignored her. "It sounds like a classic symbiotic relationship. Morton gave Ms. Jones the exposure she needed to further her career, and having a glamorous escort no doubt lent old Clive a certain cachet. You didn't happen to ask her what she thought about her companion's laddish lifestyle, did you?"

"She knew about it all right. Said what he did on his own time was his business. But when I asked her about his drug use, she clammed right up. I was able to find out that they were out for dinner together the night he was murdered. She says that they parted company when they left the restaurant in Covent Garden and she has no idea where he went after that. She also claims she has no idea who might have done for him."

"Did you believe her?"

"No reason not to, sir."

Powell nodded. "Now it's your turn, Evans."

She glared at him. "I was going to get started yesterday evening, sir, but I got detained."

He smiled brightly. "I'll overlook it this time, provided you make up for it today. I'd like you to delve a bit more deeply into Tess Morgan and her resident's association."

"Yes, sir," she said between clenched teeth.

"You carry on with Morton, Bill, and see if you can dredge up anything else on him. And we need to see if we can trace his movements from Saturday night, when he was at the Fitzrovia, up to his murder."

Black nodded.

"I forgot to mention it earlier, but I had a most interesting chat with a chap named Les Wilkes at a sex club in Rupert Street last night."

"A sex club?" Evans asked.

"Research, Evans, research."

"The sacrifices we make," she remarked dryly.

"Old Les is a bit of a snout," Powell continued. "There isn't much that goes on in Soho he doesn't know about. To make a long story short, it seems that Clive Morton was a mainstay of the local economy. According to Wilkes, he had a thousand-pound-a-week cocaine habit."

"Maybe Dockside wasn't the only thing he and Richard Brighton had in common," Black observed.

Powell smiled grimly. "We know they probably share the same killer. Just to be on the safe side, it's probably best that I break the news to Paul Atherton and Charles Mansfield."

An hour later, Powell found himself once again in the offices of Paul Atherton in Bermondsey. The enchanting Ms. Kelly escorted him as before into Atherton's office. The developer looked surprised to see him.

"Chief Superintendent, this *is* an unexpected pleasure."

"I apologize for not calling ahead, but something has come up and I thought I should talk to you as soon as possible."

"Yes, of course." A look of concern creased his face.

"You'll recall the last time I was here, I raised the possibility of a connection between the murders of Richard Brighton and Clive Morton . . ."

Atherton nodded.

"There now seems little doubt that they were killed by the same person." Powell watched Atherton's reaction closely.

Atherton frowned. "I'm not sure I understand . . ."

Powell gave him a summary of the forensic case put together by Sir Reggie.

Atherton did not speak for a few moments. "What do think it means?" he asked eventually.

"I was hoping you could tell me, Mr. Atherton."

The developer's expression evinced an air of puzzlement. "I still don't understand. If someone was so determined to stop Dockside—I assume that's the inference one is supposed to make from all of this—wouldn't it have been easier just to get rid of *me*? It's true that Richard Brighton actively supported the project, but it's not as if he were the only one. And as you know, Clive Morton was only a small player in the scheme of things."

"My thoughts exactly," Powell agreed.

"I'm at a complete loss, Chief Superintendent."

And now to broach a potentially delicate subject. "Something else rather odd has come up. We got a call yesterday from a man claiming to know something about Dockside. He alleged that Charles Mansfield, the local Conservative councillor, stood to benefit financially from the project." He left the rest unsaid.

Atherton looked at him. "What exactly are you suggesting?"

"I'm not suggesting anything. I simply want to confirm that Clive Morton was the only other person besides yourself with a financial stake in the project."

"Very well, Chief Superintendent," he said stiffly, "I will confirm it for you. And in case you have any doubts about the matter, I can assure you that bribing politicians is not my style."

"Do you have any idea who would make such an accusation?" Powell asked patiently.

Atherton's jaw tightened. "I have my suspicions. But I'm not going to lower myself to their level by bandying about unsubstantiated allegations."

"I understand there has been considerable organized opposition to Dockside," Powell ventured. "The council tenants that are directly affected—the group led by Tess Morgan, for instance."

"My battle has never been with the tenants, Chief Superintendent. I have simply put forward a proposal to the elected representatives of the borough to develop a derelict piece of property. It is the politicians who are ultimately responsible for deciding what is in the best interests of their constituents. Unfortunately, Ms. Morgan doesn't seem to see it that way."

"What to you mean?"

"I have had to endure personal attacks from her and her group as well as chronic vandalism at the warehouse site." He hesitated. "I've also received a number of anonymous threats."

Powell gave him a sharp look. "What kind of threats?"

"Telephone calls late at night advising me to pull the plug on Dockside—or else. That sort of thing."

"A man or a woman?"

"A man, I think, although the voice was heavily disguised."

"Why didn't you tell me about this before?"

Atherton shrugged. "I didn't think it was important until now. I wasn't particularly worried—abuse goes with the territory. People often react irrationally when they are faced with change, Chief Superintendent."

"That's as may be, Mr. Atherton, but uttering a threat is a criminal offense," Powell said, an edge of impatience in his voice. "Now I want you to think about this carefully: When was the first time you received such a threat?"

Atherton frowned thoughtfully. "Two or three months ago, I think."

"That was before Richard Brighton's murder."

Atherton nodded.

"When was the last time?"

Atherton shifted awkwardly in his chair. "A few days before Clive was killed," he said.

Powell exploded. "How could you be so bloody stupid? This is potentially important evidence, not to mention the fact that your own life may well be at risk."

The developer looked embarrassed. "I'm sorry, Chief Superintendent. I realize I was wrong not to tell you. My only excuse is I've been under a lot of stress lately, and I—" He stopped himself. "In any case, I assure you it won't happen again."

Powell sighed. "All right, Mr. Atherton. Is there anything else you want to tell me?"

"This is a bit awkward, but this, er, spurious allegation concerning Charles Mansfield—if it got out, it might create the wrong impression. I mean, the support for Dockside is tenuous enough as it is . . ."

"You can rest assured that the police won't be saying anything about it. That would just play into the hands of the perpetrator, wouldn't it?"

Atherton looked relieved. "Thank you, Chief Superintendent."

"Where is your residence, Mr. Atherton?"

He glanced up at the ceiling. "I have a flat upstairs. I also spend weekends at my partner's place in Marylebone. She has an apartment in Portland Place."

"You may wish to start taking precautions," Powel advised in a flat voice. "I don't wish to alarm you unduly, but until we know exactly what we're dealing with, if it were me, I'd assume the worst."

Atherton nodded soberly. "I could move in with Susan, I suppose."

"That might be wise. I'd appreciate it if you could let me know."

"Of course."

Powell rose to his feet. "Don't hesitate to call me day or night if anything should come up."

"Thank you, Chief Superintendent."

"Take care of yourself, Mr. Atherton."

As Powell left the developer's office, he had the disconcerting sense of being trapped on a runaway train that was on the verge of careening off the tracks.

CHAPTER 20

"It's utterly preposterous!" Charles Mansfield sputtered. "I'll sue the bugger for all he's worth!"

"That might be an option if we knew who he was, Mr. Mansfield," Powell pointed out.

Mansfield stared out the floor-to-ceiling window in his office at the broad sweep of the Thames and the gleaming towers of the City beyond him. "Politics is a dirty business, Chief Superintendent, a dirty business indeed." He did not elaborate.

"To put your mind at ease, Mr. Mansfield, I have already come to the conclusion that the allegation is untrue. I am, however, interested in the motivation of the person who made it. I can only assume at this point that it was intended to undermine support for Dockside. I'm wondering what you think."

Mansfield turned to look at him. "Your guess is as good as mine, Chief Superintendent."

Powell persisted. "I understand that the project has enjoyed a resurgence of support since Richard Brighton's

141

death. Do you think the call might have something to do with that?"

"It's ironic, isn't it?" Mansfield said. "When Dockside is eventually built, Richard will get all the credit for it. They'll probably erect a bloody commemorative plaque," he added bitterly. "I've supported the project since day one, and unlike some of its fair-weather friends, I've never wavered in my commitment. And what bloody thanks do I get? Hints and allegations clearly intended to besmirch my reputation and damage me politically. Well, I won't stand for it!" His face reddened. "I will not sit back and allow everything I've worked for be destroyed. I refuse to be relegated to some political backwater for the rest—" He checked himself. "Forgive me, Chief Superintendent, but as I'm sure you can appreciate, I am justifiably out-raged by this lie."

"Quite. But let's not beat about the bush, Mr. Mans-field. You must have some idea who is responsible."

Mansfield's expression darkened. "Oh, I know who's behind it all right."

Powell waited.

"I'm going to handle this in my own way, Chief Superintendent."

"Be sensible, Mr. Mansfield. Until we know who placed that call, we're powerless to stop him."

This caught the councillor's attention. "Stop him? What do you mean?"

"We have reason to believe that Richard Brighton and Clive Morton, the restaurant critic, were murdered by the same person."

"What's it got to do with me?" Mansfield asked edgily.

"The one thing they appear to have in common is Dockside. Brighton was its main political booster, and we've recently discovered that Morton had a financial interest in the project." He paused significantly. "You are also a prominent supporter, Mr. Mansfield, and until we know better, I think it would be prudent to assume that you could also be at risk."

He looked incredulous. "Surely you're not suggesting that *my* life is in danger?"

"I don't know what to think at this point. That's why I'm asking for your bloody help," Powell snapped. "The fact remains that Richard Brighton was brutally assaulted then thrown into the Thames to drown and Clive Morton had his throat cut."

Mansfield smiled. "I appreciate your interest in my welfare, Chief Superintendent, but I can look after myself, don't you worry."

Powell could barely contain his frustration. "I can't force you to tell me, Mr. Mansfield," he said crisply, getting to his feet. "If you change your mind, you know where to find me."

It was curious, Powell thought as he walked across London Bridge to Monument Station, that Charles Mansfield seemed more concerned about his political survival than the prospect of being murdered.

When Powell got back to the Yard, feeling peckish, frustrated, and irritable, Detective-Sergeant Black was waiting for him.

"There was another phone call, sir, just a few minutes ago. It may have been the same bloke, but I can't be sure." He paused significantly.

Powell sighed. "Get on with it, Black."

"Yes, sir. He said that we might want to look into Adrian Turner's relationship with Richard Brighton's widow."

"What?"

"Apparently they've been seen together recently. Our caller suggested in so many words that, with her husband out of the way, Mrs. Brighton was, er, ripe for the picking, you might say."

"Were you able to trace the call this time?"

"Yes, sir. It came from a call box in London Bridge Station."

Powell thought about this for a moment. "There is something not right about this, Black. Or perhaps I'm simply suffering from low blood sugar. I'm going to lunch."

Celia Cross was presiding over the bar at the Fitzrovia Tavern. She smiled toothily when he walked in. "What'll it be, Mr. Powell?"

"The usual, I think, Celia. No word from Jill, I take it?" he asked as she filled his glass.

She shook her head forlornly. "It's been over a week. I'm beginning to give up 'ope."

"The Missing Persons Bureau has put out a press release across the country. I'm hopeful that something will come of it." He tried to create an impression of confidence. "Has our friend the poet shown his face here lately?"

The publican scowled. " 'E wouldn't dare!"

"You mentioned before that Clive Morton was here on the night that Snavely tried to follow Jill home. He didn't come back the next day, by any chance? Or on Monday?"

She shook her head. "No, I would remember that because of the way 'e carried on with Jill."

"Apart from being generally obnoxious that night, is there anything else that struck you about him—anything he said or did?"

She frowned. "Can't say as I noticed anything in particular . . . Just a tick! I do recall something. After 'e first came in, 'e acted as if 'e was waiting for someone."

"What do you mean?"

"You know, constantly checking 'is watch, looking when people walked in the door, that sort of thing."

"How long did that go on for?"

"I dunno, fifteen minutes maybe. Then people began drifting over to 'is table."

"People?"

"There were three or four of 'em. I recognized a couple of newspaper types that come in from time to time."

"Could one of them have been the person Morton was waiting for?"

She looked thoughtful. "I don't know why really, but I don't think so. They were more casual encounters, like."

"How long was Morton here?"

" 'E came in around ten, I think, so about an hour and a half."

"What time did Jill leave?"

"It was after eleven. I remember it was just before closing time, so I wasn't too worried about it."

"What about Snavely?"

She frowned. "I just can't remember. I know 'e was 'ere earlier, but it was fairly busy, so I wasn't paying attention."

Powell smiled reassuringly. "Tell me again what happened next."

"The poor girl came running in about ten minutes later, panting and sobbing and scared 'alf to death. She managed to tell me what happened, and I called the police. They got 'ere a few minutes later and cleared everybody out."

"That would have been going on eleven-thirty, I imagine."

She nodded.

"Do you recall if Morton was here when the police arrived?"

"I—I think so, but I can't be sure. I was too busy worrying about Jill to pay any attention to the likes of 'im."

"Then what happened?"

"The police took a statement from Jill and left. I fixed her a hot drink, we talked for a while, then I called 'er a cab. I tried to get 'er to come 'ome with me, but she wouldn't 'ere of it." Celia's eyes glistened. "If she 'ad, maybe she'd still be 'ere."

"Don't torture yourself, Celia," Powell said gently. "I'm convinced that Jill left of her own accord for her own reasons. The only thing that has me puzzled is why she didn't tell anyone where she was going. She doesn't strike me as the type who would needlessly worry her friends."

Celia sniffed. "I like to think I'm 'er friend."

"Of course you are." Powell drained his pint while his hostess filled another glass for him. "Now I'd like you to tell me exactly what Jill told you about what happened to her that night."

Celia described Jill's panicked flight from Windmill Street into Colville Place, how she had stumbled and fallen to the pavement and just barely made it back to the pub with her pursuer hot on her heels. The publican smiled ever so slightly. "She said she nearly bowled over some poor bloke with a gammy leg standing outside the pub. After that, it's all just a blur, I'm afraid."

"Thank you, Celia. You've been most helpful. Now then—" he rubbed his hands briskly together "—I'll have the fish and chips and damn the cholesterol."

CHAPTER 21

That evening found Powell pacing restlessly back and forth in the flat in Lexington Street, chain-smoking and listening to an old Jeff Beck record from Tony Osborne's blues collection, wondering what to do with himself. In a moment of weakness he even debated whether or not to watch the billiards championships on BBC2. Mercifully, his mindless deliberations were interrupted by the telephone ringing.

The familiar voice at the other end caused a shock to surge through his body. He listened numbly.

"It's me. Jill."

Silence.

"I called the Yard and your assistant, Sergeant Black, gave me your number."

"Where the hell have you been?" he suddenly exploded. "We've all been worried half to death!"

"I—I don't understand—" She sounded confused.

"You've got some explaining to do, young lady," he said sternly. "Where are you now?"

"In Paddington."

He checked his watch. "Look, I'll meet you at Starbucks in forty-five minutes. All right?"

"Yes, fine . . . Powell, I'm sorry for all this. I had no idea . . . I mean, I'll try to explain when I see you."

An awkward pause followed.

"Jill . . ."

"Yes?"

"Are you all right?"

She hesitated. "I'm okay."

"Right, I'll see you in a bit."

She rang off abruptly.

Powell felt a wave of relief wash over him, diluting the sense of anger at what could only be interpreted as highly irresponsible behavior. Ever since she had disappeared, a bitter draft of morbid possibilities involving Simon Snavely and even Clive Morton had been bubbling away, just barely under the surface, in his mind's ferment. The main thing was she was back and he had one less thing to distract him. He downed his Scotch and turned off the record player. As he locked the door behind him, he couldn't help noticing that Tony's flowers were looking a little limp.

He arrived at the coffeehouse a few minutes before eight. Eschewing the caffé mochas, caramel macchiatos, and double low-fat lattés in favor of a huge cup of something strong and black, he selected a seat near the window where he could watch the comings and goings in Shaftesbury Avenue. The street was alive with

colored lights and honking taxis and last-minute theatergoers rushing to their shows. It occurred to him that
he hadn't seen a play since Marion had gone away, although he supposed that he got more than his share of
comedy and tragedy every day at work. Wasn't it Sopho-
cles who wrote a play about the irresistible urge to
murder one's superior?

There was suddenly a reflection in the window. He
turned.

It was Jill, looking a little lost. "Hi," she said in a
small voice.

It was hard to know what to say. "Can I get you something?" he said.

She smiled weakly. "No, thanks, I'm coffeed-out."
She sat down across from him. "After I talked to you,"
she began before he could say anything, "I rang Stephen
to ask him why he hadn't told Celia I was going away—"

"You mean he knew?" Powell interrupted.

She nodded. "I left a note. I told him I needed to get
away to think things through. I asked him to let Celia
know that I wouldn't be able to work for a while. I felt
badly about it at the time, but I knew she'd understand."
She hesitated. "Something happened on my last night at
work . . ."

"Celia told me about it," Powell said gently.

She stared out the window at her own reflection.
"Stephen was so angry, he tore up the note without
telling anyone about it." She looked into Powell's eyes.
"You can't imagine how badly I feel about all of this.
Poor Celia must have been frantic. I tried to ring you

from the train station before I left, but I couldn't get through."

Powell felt a twinge of guilt for not taking her call that morning. Moreover, it seemed likely that the vindictive behavior of Jill's boyfriend had been precipitated, at least in part, by his own irresponsible behavior. If he hadn't had considerably more than sufficient one night and used Jill's flat as a hotel, perhaps none of this would have happened.

"It was you who got me thinking," Jill was saying.

Powell groaned inwardly, bracing himself for the worst.

"You told me to follow my heart, remember? You helped me see what an empty existence I was leading. I had a boyfriend who was using me, a job that exposed me to abuse and harassment, and more than anything else, I realized I was homesick."

"I didn't say follow your heart, exactly," Powell protested weakly. He felt more like an accomplice in some sordid little peccadillo than someone in a position to be giving advice.

"Don't be so modest, Powell," Jill rejoined with a flash of her old spirit. "If it hadn't been for you, I'd still be stuck in the same old rut. As it is, my only regret is that I worried my friends."

"Where did you go?" he asked, somewhat deflated.

"Northumberland. I ended up in a little seaside town called Alnmouth near Alnwick. Do you know it?"

He nodded.

"I stayed at a charming bed-and-breakfast with English breakfasts and a cozy fire at night, long walks on the sand, and no one to tell me what do to—just oodles of time to read and think. I was being selfish, I know, but it was exhilarating and liberating at the same time." She searched his face for a glimmer of understanding. "Do you know what I mean, Powell?"

He sighed. "Yes, Jill, I know what you mean."

She regarded him with an expression of concern, searching for the right words. "I know you feel guilty about what happened that night. If Stephen wants to fly off in a jealous rage, that's his problem. I never want to see him again."

An appropriate response eluded him. "Why did you decide to come back now?"

She flushed. "I heard a bulletin about me this morning on the radio. A Canadian girl, Jill Burroughs, reported missing, et cetera. I was mortified, as you can imagine. I'd purposely avoided newspapers and listening to the news, so it came as quite a shock. I called the local police to let them know I was all right. When I was unable to get in touch with Stephen to find out what was going on, I rushed back to London as quickly as I could."

"What will you do now?" Powell asked.

She shrugged. "It will be hard to go back to the Fitzrovia after all that's happened."

"You might be interested to know I had a little chat with your secret admirer, Simon Snavely."

A blank look on her face.

"The poet."

Her eyes widened. "Oh, my God, you caught him?"

"Not exactly. He's the one who followed you, all

right. He maintains, however, that he only intended to present you with his latest collection of poems, dedicated to you."

She screwed up her face. "That guy is weird. Are you going to charge him or something?"

"That rather depends on you."

"What do you mean?"

"Are you willing to bring forward a formal complaint?"

"He *did* scare me half to death . . . I don't know. What do you think I should do?"

"The question is did he intend to threaten or harm you? It might be difficult to prove, coming down in the end to his word against yours. As an accused person, he would of course receive the benefit of any doubt."

Jill appeared to consider this. "I suppose you're right. But I don't see how I could go back to working at the pub with him skulking about."

"Do you want to go back?"

She frowned. "I don't suppose I do, really. Actually, I've been thinking about going home. There's nothing to keep me here now. I've been away for nearly two years, and I think it's about time I decided what I want to do with my life."

Powell nodded. Ah, to be young, footloose, and fancy free again. Jill struck him as a sensible young woman who knew her mind and would undoubtedly make the right decision. Certainly Stephen Potter was no loss. He was taking a sip of his coffee when something suddenly occurred to him. "You've heard about Clive Morton, I expect."

She looked puzzled. "The restaurant critic?"

Powell nodded. "He was found murdered in Soho the morning after you left."

She looked as if she had seen a ghost. "What—what happened?"

"It wasn't very pleasant. Someone cut his throat."

She stared at him, her face expressionless. "He was in the pub Saturday night. I didn't like him very much."

"I understand he'd been bothering you."

She swallowed. "I don't feel very well. I think I should be going."

"Of course. Where are you staying?"

"At a hotel. Near Paddington Station."

"I'll walk you to the tube."

She stood up. "No, I'll be fine. I need to clear my head. Goodbye, Powell, and . . . thanks for everything."

Then she turned abruptly and walked out the door, merging into the stream of passersby. Well, that's that, Powell thought as he drained his cup. He had no way of knowing how wrong he was.

CHAPTER 22

The next morning, Detective-Sergeant Black made arrangements to meet Samantha Jones at a video production studio in Wardour Street. She was working apparently and agreed to spare him ten minutes during her morning break.

He inquired at the reception desk and was directed to the cafeteria downstairs. He located her at the far end at a table with two muscular and unseasonably tanned young men, who Black assumed were models as well.

"Get lost, boys, it's the cops," she said laconically when he approached their table.

The two men scattered. She tossed her long black hair and crossed her legs. She was wearing a skintight, black vinyl bodysuit adorned with metal studs that left little to the imagination. "Take a load off your feet, Sergeant."

He tried not to stare. "Yes, er, thank you, miss." He settled himself carefully on one of the molded plastic

155

chairs. "Doing some modeling this morning?" he asked by way of making small talk.

She smiled archly. "You could say that, Sergeant. More of an educational video, really. And we're shooting the, um, climax of the piece in about fifteen minutes, so if you don't mind . . ."

"Yes, of course, miss. This shouldn't take long. You mentioned when we last spoke that you accompanied Clive Morton to a restaurant on the Monday evening before he was killed."

"Yes, he was doing a review on the Golden Quail in Covent Garden. I thought it was marvelous, but of course Clive hated it."

"Did anything out of the ordinary happen when you were there?"

"You mean apart from Clive carrying on and making a complete arse of himself as usual?"

"Yes, miss, if you like. Apart from that."

She shrugged. "Not that I can recall . . . Wait a minute, he *was* called away to the phone, but he didn't say who it was. It was just before we left."

"What time did you leave the restaurant?"

"I can't remember exactly."

"Could you try, miss? It's important. We know from the pathologist's report that Mr. Morton was murdered sometime between eleven-forty-five Monday night and a quarter past twelve Tuesday morning, so it's important that we trace his movements up to that point."

She frowned as if in deep concentration. "I don't know . . . It must have been between eleven and eleven-thirty. I remember I got home just before midnight."

"Did he say anything about meeting someone else?"

Her dark eyes flashed. "Not in so many words, but I wouldn't have put it past him."

"What do you mean, miss?"

"You must know enough about Clive by now that I don't have to draw you a picture."

"You didn't like him much, did you?"

"I don't think about it in those terms. This business is all about self-promotion, Sergeant. Love him or hate him, Clive Morton was a well-known personality in this town, and being seen with him helped raise my profile. End of story." She looked slightly uncomfortable. "I still have to do things I don't particularly like, but it won't be long before I'll be calling the shots. I hope I haven't shocked you, Sergeant."

"It's not for me to judge, Miss Jones. Getting back to the night in question, you're sure he didn't say where he was going after he left you?"

"I told you—I'm sure. It was getting late. I told him I had to go. We left the restaurant together, and that was the last time I saw him. What he did after that was his business."

"Oh, he did some business with someone all right, and he left an odd sort of calling card."

"What do you mean?"

"It's not common knowledge, miss, but the person who slit his throat and left him to bleed to death stuffed an apple in his mouth." He paused for effect. "As a sort of garnish, like."

She shuddered. "What sort of animal would do something like that?"

"I was hoping you could tell me, miss."

She shook her head in exasperation. "I told you before, I don't have a clue—" She hesitated. "Unless . . ."

"Yes, miss?"

"It sounds ridiculous, but I wonder if Clive could have pissed someone off to the point where . . . I mean, his restaurant reviews were getting more and more *out there*, if you know what I mean."

"Do you have anyone in mind?"

"Not really. You could check his newspaper columns, I suppose—I never read his stuff myself." She glanced significantly at the wall clock. "I'm sorry, but I'm on in a few minutes and I should get, um, warmed up." She smiled. "Would you care to stay and watch?"

Sergeant Black flushed profusely. "Er, no, thank you, miss. I'd better be off." He mumbled a goodbye and fled the cafeteria.

Powell sat in Adrian Turner's tiny office in a lane off Tooley Street, a five-minute walk from the cafe where they had first met. It consisted of one room, one desk and computer, one file cabinet, and three posters—one on each of the dingy inside walls—depicting clear-cutting in British Columbia, soil erosion in Nepal, and a large pipe discharging some sort of black liquid into an inhospitable-looking body of water. Aside from representing his constituents on Southwark Council, Powell wondered what Turner actually did for a living.

The councillor was obviously not happy. "You think I made the frigging phone call? See here, Chief Superintendent, I have absolutely no respect for Charles Mansfield or anything he stands for, but that doesn't mean I'd sink to his level and start making personal attacks, let alone anonymous phone calls to the police about his financial dealings."

"So you deny accusing him of having a conflict of interest over Dockside?"

Turner scowled. "I told you."

"All right, but do you think there could be any truth to the allegation?"

"How the hell would I know? Mind you, I wouldn't put anything past him. His type always considers his own interests above everything else."

"Just for the sake of argument," Powell persisted, "if you did become aware that a fellow councillor had an undisclosed financial interest in a matter that was under consideration by the council, what would you do?"

"I would do my duty, Chief Superintendent, and bring it to the attention of the council."

"Duty? Independent of any political advantage?"

"I didn't say that."

"Please bear with me, Mr. Turner. I'm trying to figure out why someone in possession of such information would go to the police rather than raise the issue in the political forum. If one of your own supporters, for instance, had the goods on a rival politician, why not just come to you and let you inflict the political damage, if that was the intent of the exercise?"

Turner regarded Powell warily. "This is all highly hypothetical, Chief Superintendent. As I just told you, I had no knowledge of any allegation against Charles Mansfield until you brought it up."

"I imagine your party will be looking for someone to take up the torch from Brighton," Powell observed casually.

"What's that supposed to mean?" Turner demanded.

"I would have thought that you would be the leading candidate to oppose Charles Mansfield and the Tories on council. However, if Mansfield were to become embroiled in some sort of political scandal . . ."

Turner smirked. "I find your heavy-handed innuendoes rather amusing. Why don't you just come out and say it, and save us both a lot of time and aggro."

"All right, Mr. Turner, I'll come out and say it. There is something funny going on, and I'm going to get to the bottom of it. Two days ago, someone accuses Charles Mansfield of improper financial dealings, then yesterday we get a call about you and Mrs. Brighton."

The color drained from Turner's face like claret from a glass. "What do you mean?"

"Why don't you tell me?"

"I know her of course—I mean, we're just acquaintances."

"Who said you were anything else?"

Without warning, Turner leapt to his feet. "My relationship with Helen Brighton, or anyone else for that matter, is my business and my business alone. I have nothing more to say. If you want to ask me any more questions, I'd like to have my solicitor present."

"As you wish, Mr. Turner," Powell said evenly. "Because I may need to talk to you again."

When Powell had gone, Turner picked up the telephone. He pressed the keys mechanically, his face taut.

The urgent double tone continued for several seconds before someone answered. He inhaled sharply. "We need to talk." He described Powell's visit in considerable detail. "It's laughable, isn't it?" he said without humor. "Who else could it be? Luckily the stupid bastard didn't get it quite right. The thing is if anyone ever found out about us, it would be very damaging—my political objectivity would be compromised, wouldn't it?" His expression darkened. "And Mansfield would have a bloody field day with it." He listened to her reply. "Right. I think that would be wise." After disconnecting, he sat motionless in his chair, staring out the rain-splattered window at the distorted image of the traffic streaming by in Tooley Street.

CHAPTER 23

After leaving Adrian Turner's office, Powell stopped in unannounced to see Charles Mansfield.

"To what do I owe this unexpected pleasure, Chief Superintendent?" Mansfield drawled, his voice thick with sarcasm.

"What the hell do you think you're playing at?" Powell exploded. "Do you think this is some kind of bloody game—an opportunity to score political points?"

Mansfield was clearly taken aback by Powell's attack. "I have no idea what you're talking about," he replied in a brittle voice. "And I must say I don't much care for your tone."

"You made that telephone call, didn't you? You insinuated that Adrian Turner is having an affair with Helen Brighton, as if anybody cared. I can only assume that you wanted us to leap to the conclusion that there must be some connection with Richard Brighton's murder. It's so bloody amateurish, it's laughable."

Mansfield's eyes narrowed. "I could say that I don't

know what you're talking about. I will say this, however: I'll not sit idly back and have my good name dragged through the mud by a whining little Trotskyite like Adrian Turner." He smiled coldly. "You're quite right, Chief Superintendent. It is a game, and one has to fight fire with fire if one is to prevail. You of all people, a policeman, should appreciate that. In your line of work, the criminal is given every advantage—you are prevented by the system from fighting back on an equal footing. Consequently, crime is running rampant in this country, and you are powerless to do anything about it."

"If you ever decide to run for prime minister," Powell commented acidly, "I'll vote for you. In the meantime, I'm going to make it my business to make your life bloody miserable."

"What the devil do you mean?"

"There are two ways of looking at it, Mr. Mansfield. Perhaps you simply suffered a lapse in judgment and allowed yourself to be drawn into a petty political vendetta. I have no doubt that you believe Adrian Turner made the phone call alleging your financial interest in Dockside. And you've more or less admitted that you feel justified in taking revenge. However, it is the alternative interpretation of your actions that interests me more."

Mansfield stared at Powell with morbid fascination, like a snake sizing up a mongoose.

"Whoever murdered Richard Brighton did you a very large favor by eliminating your chief political rival and, as an added bonus, enabling you to claim credit for Dockside if and when it eventually gets the green light.

All that remained for you to do was to come up with some way to discredit Adrian Turner, thereby virtually assuring your selection as mayor next year. And then on to bigger and better things, no doubt. The question is, Are you simply a tenant in this glittering tower of political opportunity or its chief architect?" Pretty thin gruel, Powell realized, but it seemed to strike a nerve.

The councillor's eyes bulged alarmingly in his pudgy, red face. "You must be bloody mad!" he sputtered.

The day was damp and dreary, unlike the previous occasion when Detective-Sergeant Evans had driven out to Rotherhithe, and despite the fact she had the car heater going full blast, she could not get warm. Across the river was her old neighborhood of Stepney, the familiar landmarks appearing indistinct and ambiguous in the mist like the memories of her East End childhood. As she pulled into the council estate car park she could not help wondering if the sympathetic feelings that admittedly clouded her assessment of Tess Morgan and her cause had something to do with her own upbringing. In many ways, Tess reminded her of her mother, fiercely independent and single-mindedly dedicated to her family. For all that, Evans considered herself an excellent judge of people and could not bring herself to believe that the community activist had anything to do with the Dockside murders. Evans knew, however, that Powell would have to be convinced. Not that there was any *particular* reason to suspect Tess Morgan—it was simply one of many possibilities that needed to be systematically considered and eliminated.

It seemed to Evans that the connection between the murders of Richard Brighton and Clive Morton and the Dockside development was unlikely to be the obvious one. This was partly because she tended to be suspicious of simplistic solutions. People and their motivations were hopelessly complex, so why should one expect the crimes they commit to be anything else? She mulled over the possibility that something else besides Dockside connected Richard Brighton and Clive Morton. Morton's alleged drug use suggested a possible avenue of investigation, and she wondered if a drug screen had been run on either of the victims as part of the postmortem investigations. She made a mental note to speak to Powell about it. However, her woman's intuition (the possession of which she would never dream of admitting to her male colleagues for fear of appearing nonanalytical) told her that drugs were too obvious. She still felt, as she had when Powell had first discussed the case with her in the cafeteria that day, that Richard Brighton was the key to the whole affair. But just how, exactly, continued to elude her. It was in this distracted frame of mind that she knocked on Tess Morgan's door.

The door opened and Ms. Morgan smiled unconvincingly. She seemed tense. "It's good to see you again, Sergeant Evans. Please come in." She ushered Evans into a small sitting room that appeared to also serve as her office. Papers, books, and magazines were piled everywhere. Occupying the far wall was a computer workstation, above which a poster depicting giant moss-covered trees proclaimed SAVE THE GREAT BEAR RAIN

FOREST. Against the adjoining wall, facing the window, was a threadbare sofa and on the wall opposite the computer desk was a shelf unit housing a television and stereo system.

"Please," she said, gesturing toward the sofa. "I'm just finishing lunch—can I get you something?"

Evans smiled. "No, thank you."

"Would you like a cup of tea?"

"Lovely," said Sergeant Evans. "I'm chilled to the bone."

As her hostess organized things in the kitchen, Evans conducted an internal debate over how to approach the task at hand. She was torn between her innate inclination to be sympathetic when conducting an interview with someone who is not actually a suspect, particularly with a person she felt some connection with, and the need at times to aggressively seek direct answers to difficult questions. On balance, she felt that the softer approach was often the more effective one, but in this case she decided that it was time to cut to the chase in order to satisfy Powell and, she admitted, to assuage her own doubts.

Tess Morgan returned with the tea things and set them on the coffee table. "I'll let you fix your own," she said.

A few moments later, Evans felt a reviving glow radiating outward from the center of her being. Nothing like a hot cup of tea, she thought contentedly, the traditional English recreational drug.

"I assume this is not a social call, Sergeant Evans," her hostess was saying.

Evans set her cup on its saucer. "No, Ms. Morgan, I'm afraid it's not. I need to ask you a few more questions. You see," she said, taking the plunge, "we keep coming back in this investigation to Richard Brighton's support for Dockside, the fact that he took an unpopular stand in some people's eyes—"

"You think I killed him," Tess said matter-of-factly.

"I didn't say that, but one has to ask the question: Could someone have been so opposed to Brighton's position on Dockside, they were prepared to take desperate measures to stop him?"

"All right, you've asked the question."

"Ms. Morgan, I understand that you represent the tenants in this block of flats. Is there some sort of residents' association?"

"There's an ad hoc committee that was organized to oppose Dockside."

"And you're the chairperson?"

"Yes."

"How many others are there on this committee?"

"Apart from me, about a half dozen regular member."

"Could you provide me a list of their names?"

"I speak for the group, Sergeant Evans—"

"I'd still like to talk to the other members," Evans persisted.

Tess nodded reluctantly.

"I have to ask this next question, Ms. Morgan: Can you think of anyone on your committee who might have had a particular ax to grind with Brighton?" It came out more awkwardly then she had intended.

Tess looked more disappointed than anything else. "We all had the same ax to grind, as you put it: the prospect of being turned out of our homes. However, we're a community action group, Sergeant Evans, not a band of bloodthirsty vigilantes."

Evans felt annoyed at herself for feeling slightly defensive. "I understand why you might be offended by my question, but the fact remains, Ms. Morgan, there is a cold-blooded murderer at large. He's killed twice already, and there's a possibility he may strike again—"

"Twice?" A puzzled look on her face.

"You must have read about Clive Morton in the papers? We haven't advertised the fact, but we have reason to believe that he was killed by the same person who murdered Richard Brighton."

If Evans had expected this revelation to evoke a reaction, she would not have been disappointed. Tess Morgan turned white as a sheet; she looked as if she were going to be sick. She swallowed. "I—I don't understand."

Evans tried to read her face. "Morton had a financial interest in Dockside," she explained. "We think that's why he was killed."

Tess did not say anything for a few seconds. When she finally spoke, her voice was oddly emotionless. "That bastard," she said. "That perverted, unspeakable bastard."

As Evans turned out of the car park onto Rotherhithe Street, she felt a bit like Pandora. Tess's reaction to the mention of Clive Morton's name was unexpected as well as inexplicable. She wondered what could possibly connect a person like Tess Morgan with the likes of Clive Morton. Whatever it was, she had a feeling she wasn't going to like the answer.

CHAPTER 24

As she drove, preoccupied, along Rotherhithe Street, Detective-Sergeant Evans noticed a redbrick schoolhouse off to her left. On the spur of the moment, she took the next turning and doubled back on a parallel side street to the school. She was directed by the secretary to the office of the headmistress, a Ms. J. S. Finlayson.

Ms. Finlayson looked up from her desk, removed her reading glasses, and regarded Evans impassively. She was a small, gray woman with penetrating eyes who exuded an air of competent efficiency.

"Sit down, Sergeant Evans."

Evans had to suppress the urge to respond with a subdued "Yes, ma'am."

"I understand that you are here about Rachel Morgan," Ms. Finlayson said.

Evans knew she was on shaky ground. "I've just come from visiting her mother—I was passing by—and it occurred to me that this might be Rachel's school."

"You guessed correctly," Ms. Finlayson observed antiseptically.

"I won't go all around the houses, Ms. Finlayson," Evans began carefully. "I'm in the process of making various inquiries related to a serious crime. At the outset, I can assure you that Rachel is not suspected of having any involvement in this crime. I simply want to ask you a few questions about her."

The headmistress eyed Evans shrewdly. "If she's not involved in anything illegal, why are you here?"

Evans smiled. "I'll be honest with you, Ms. Finlayson. I'm not quite sure why I'm here. Call it woman's intuition. The thing is—" she hesitated "—I'm wondering if Rachel Morgan has ever had any problem with drugs."

Ms. Finlayson did not speak for a few moments. "You should be aware, Sergeant Evans," she said eventually in a dry voice, "that I am constrained by requirements of confidentiality in such matters. Furthermore, I dislike fishing expeditions on the part of the police. The children in this area have enough problems without being persecuted simply for who they are and where they happen to live."

Evans blushed. "Believe me, that is not my intent. I know as well as anyone—" She checked herself.

"Yes, Sergeant Evans?"

"I can't force you to talk to me about Rachel, Ms. Finlayson."

The headmistress frowned. "You said that you just came from visiting her mother. Is she in some sort of trouble?"

"I don't think so," Evans replied honestly.

"Pleased don't misunderstand me, Sergeant Evans, if you had a legitimate reason for your interest in Rachel, I might view things differently. However, as things stand, I am afraid I can't help you."

Evans sighed. "I haven't been completely honest with you, Ms. Finlayson. The crime I referred to is murder, and the victim is known to have been involved with drugs. I am concerned that there may be other victims in this case, victims of drug abuse, who may have been influenced by this person."

The headmistress regarded her speculatively. "This is all very cryptic. However, I sense that you are motivated by concern for Rachel's welfare, so I am prepared to tell you this much. Rachel has had her share of problems, but I believe that she has put them behind her. She is quite a creative girl—she wants to be a artist, you know—but, unfortunately, she spent too much time last term hanging about in Soho getting into the sort of trouble that young people seem to get into these days. Without putting too fine a point on it, I can tell you that the poor girl went through some very dark days, some very dark days indeed. And, yes, drugs were involved. However, with her mother's help, she's managed to straighten herself out and has been applying herself at school this term. Rachel is a good girl, Sergeant Evans, and I have every confidence that she will make something of herself."

Looking back on it, Evans did not remember thanking the headmistress, walking out of the Rotherhithe Comprehensive School, or even getting into her car. Her first recollection was driving across Westminster Bridge and being struck by the realization that she may have just unearthed a plausible motive for Clive Morton's murder.

Powell bumped into Evans in the Back Hall on his way out of the building. "You don't look too good," he remarked.

"Thanks," she said sourly. "I need to talk to you—"

"Can it wait until tomorrow morning? I've made arrangements to see Mrs. Brighton this afternoon."

"Right, tomorrow morning." She hesitated. "Would you mind if I gave Sir Reggie a call? I'd like to have a drug screen run on both Morton and Brighton."

Powell smiled. "It's your funeral." He turned to leave.

"Sir?"

"Yes, Evans?"

"Sergeant Black told me about your friend, Jill Burroughs. I'm glad."

He looked at her with a curious expression on his face. "Some stories do have happy endings. Take it to heart, Evans."

After a cheese sandwich and limp salad in the cafeteria, she went back to her office and wrote down a list of points she wished to discuss with Sir Reginald Quick. She steeled herself for a few moments, then placed the call.

The pathologist answered on the first ring. "Quick," he barked ambiguously.

Evans promptly introduced herself.

A brief pause. "Ah, yes, the Yorkshire moors affair. I remember you, Sergeant Evans. You were a damn sight better company than your superior, I can tell you that. I nearly caught my death on that outing," he muttered. "Now, then, what can I do for you?"

"I was wondering, Sir Reginald—"

There was an ominous rumble on the other end of the line.

"Sorry, er, Reggie. I was wondering whether any drug tests were done as part of the Brighton and Morton postmortems."

"Drug tests? You'll have to be more specific."

"Oh, you know, alcohol and the usual blood screen for illicit drugs," she replied lamely.

A rustling of papers. "Let me see . . . Brighton was checked for alcohol, as is usual in cases of drowning in which it could be a contributing factor. There was alcohol in his blood, but the concentration was relatively low, equivalent to a glass or two of wine. No tests were done on Morton as far as I can see, but the cause of death in his case was, er, rather clear-*cut*. Ha ha!"

Evans chuckled politely. "What about cocaine—can you test for that?"

Sir Reggie grunted in the affirmative. "It can be readily detected with an immunoassay, followed by quantification using GC-MS, er, gas chromatography and mass spectroscopy. *If,* that is, there is ample justification for doing so. It comes down to an assessment by the pathologist of the cost of the analysis versus the potential benefit to be derived. As I am sure you are aware,

Sergeant Evans, we live in difficult budgetary times," he added austerely.

"Would blood samples from both victims have been retained?"

"In homicide cases, samples are kept for six months in the event that further analysis is required."

"Would it be possible then to have both victims' blood tested for cocaine?"

"There is a small problem with that: Cocaine and its metabolites are unstable in blood, so it's not likely you'd find anything."

"Oh," Evans said, the disappointment sounding in her voice.

"However," he continued mischievously, "it can be detected in urine, samples of which were taken in both cases. But, as I said a moment ago, you'd first have to convince me to order the tests."

Evans could visualize Sir Reggie's carnivorous grin. She gave the pathologist a rundown on Morton's alleged cocaine abuse and the importance of exploring any possible links between him and Brighton.

"Powell didn't tell me any of this!" the pathologist roared. "How the hell are we supposed to know what to look for if we don't have the complete picture?"

Evans did her best to defend her superior's honor, explaining that the information about Morton's drug use had only recently come to light. Sir Reggie did not seem entirely convinced. "Nonetheless, I will order the tests," he said grudgingly. "I should have the results tomorrow afternoon."

"Thanks, Reggie. You're a dear," she said, emboldened by her success.

The pathologist mumbled something unintelligible and rang off.

CHAPTER 25

Powell stepped out of Sloane Square tube station into the afternoon sunlight. The paved square with its Venus fountain and plane trees, in spring bud that day, was basically a glorified roundabout collecting traffic from Knightsbridge, the King's Road, and Pimlico. Once a tiny fishing hamlet on the Thames, in the last century the old village of Chelsea became a thriving colony of literary and artistic talent, including the likes of Carlyle, Whistler, and Oscar Wilde. A revival of sorts occurred in the Swinging Sixties when rock stars and other celebrities of the day converged on the trendy boutiques and coffee bars that lined the King's Road.

As property values soared in recent years, the Bohemian spirit of the place inevitably withered, and Chelsea is now perhaps best known as the home of the young upper-class Sloane Rangers, with their smart-casual country outfits from Peter Jones, bright bijou-terraced homes, and glossy magazine conformity in every aspect of life from the decor of their drawing rooms to their ski holiday destinations.

As Powell set off down the King's Road, once the private route for royalty traveling from Whitehall Palace to Hampton Court and other royal retreats farther to the west, past the line of shops, trattorias, bistros, and pubs, it occurred to him that the main artery of Chelsea had at least escaped the tat of Carnaby Street and had moved on from the hippie era and the punk period. It still managed to retain a certain vibrancy, as well as an indefinable sense of *village* despite the fact that you won't find a baker or a butcher's shop.

He soon located Helen Brighton's Inner Harmony interior design shop. She was occupied with a customer, so he browsed mindlessly amongst the wallpaper and draperies.

"Can I interest you in something?"

He turned around to face Mrs. Brighton. "My wife is always telling me I have absolutely no sense of style," he replied wryly.

She laughed. "You're the best kind of customer then." She glanced around. "Why don't we go somewhere where we can talk?"

"Fine."

They bought coffees to take away at the cafe next door, then walked to a leafy square around the corner. They settled themselves on one of the wooden benches that lined the square around a central blaze of orange and yellow tulips, and Powell asked her how long she had had the shop.

"About ten years now. I owned it before I met Richard.

It used to be a fashion boutique back then, but these days *feng shui* is much hotter than miniskirts."

"I hear they've rearranged the furniture at Number Ten in order to energize the PM," Powell observed dryly.

"You might be interested to know I was the one who advised Tony and Cherie Blair to rearrange their furniture, as you put it, to promote tranquility and harmony." Her eyes sparkled mischievously. "I also advised the PM to put a fish tank in his office: three goldfish for finances and two dark fish, loaches preferably, to look after his health and the health of the nation. It is good to have movement in an office, Chief Superintendent. It stimulates mental activity."

Powell could not help but be impressed by her clientele, if not her New Age sensibilities. "I'll keep it in mind," he said, regarding her with a renewed interest. There was a vitality in her manner that had been absent on the occasion of their first meeting.

"I expect you're wondering how an interior design consultant ended up marrying a politician," she said.

He smiled. "The thought *had* crossed my mind."

"My father was the Member of Parliament for this constituency in the Callaghan years, so I literally grew up in the Labour Party. I met Richard at a party convention in 'ninety-two. The rest, as they say, is history."

"Mrs. Brighton," he began, having dispensed with the preliminaries, "you are no doubt wondering why I'm bothering you again. I'm afraid we haven't made a tremendous amount of progress in your husband's case, and I'm hoping you can help me fill in a few of the blanks."

She hesitated, then appeared to come to a decision. "Before we begin," she said, "I have a confession to make. When we first spoke at my flat, you may have sensed that I wasn't exactly thrilled with the prospect of Scotland Yard getting involved in the investigation of Richard's death. In a strange way, I found it rather frightening. It's not that I didn't want desperately to find out what happened to my husband, to have some sort of closure. It's just that—I don't know—I suppose I preferred to believe that he was a victim of some random, senseless act rather than something more sinister. Am I making any sense?"

"Perfect sense, Mrs. Brighton."

"Anyway, I've come to accept the absolute importance of getting to the truth about Richard's death, however unpleasant it may turn out to be. I'll do whatever I can to help."

Powell briefly summarized the results of the investigation to date. "The question I keep coming back to," he concluded, "is what connection could your husband possibly have had with Clive Morton other than the fact that they were both involved in quite different ways with Dockside?"

She looked mystified. "None that I can think of. I'm not even sure that Richard was aware of Morton's interest in the project. If he was, he never mentioned it to me."

Powell had feared as much. "Would you mind if we went back to the beginning of your husband's involvement with Dockside? I must admit that it continues to strike me as odd that a local Labour politician would support a project that would result in the eviction of a hundred or more council tenants."

She sighed. "I wouldn't be being entirely honest if I told you that he didn't have doubts about it. Whatever else one might say about Richard, he was deeply committed to the welfare of the working people in Southwark. But he was also a realist. It is a deplorable fact, Chief Superintendent, that due to years of neglect, the borough needs to spend nearly a billion pounds to repair and upgrade its rotting, leaking council housing. That kind of money will never be forthcoming from the central government, so the council has been forced to consider other options, such as selling off its more valuable housing near the Thames to pay for upgrading the rest. In the case of Dockside, Richard felt that the project struck an acceptable balance, although I can tell you he lost a considerable amount of sleep over the plight of the tenants. It is not widely known, but Richard negotiated a deal with the developer to reduce the commercial component of the project so as to save one of the council blocks from demolition."

"If you don't mind me asking, did you agree with your husband's position on Dockside?"

She looked at him with an odd expression on her face. "No, I didn't, actually. But then I'm not a politician. Richard was convinced that it was the right thing to do."

"The right thing or the expedient thing, Mrs. Brighton?"

"Is there a difference? To do anything in politics, Chief Superintendent, you first have to get elected."

"Point taken. However, you did mention that your

husband had some doubts about the project. Would you say that his views changed over time?"

"I think he was becoming increasingly receptive to the concerns of the local residents. There's a well-organized group representing the council tenants—"

"The one led by Tess Morgan?"

Helen Brighton nodded. "She's a very determined woman."

"She has a lot to lose."

"Yes, Chief Superintendent, she does."

"I understand that the council was divided over the matter."

She pulled a face. "That's the understatement of the year. Richard was getting it from both sides—from his own party as well as the opposition."

"From Adrian Turner and Charles Mansfield, you mean?"

"In the main, yes."

"Why don't we start with Mr. Turner? I don't imagine the party was too thrilled when an internecine squabble erupted over a high-profile project like Dockside."

"Is that a question or a statement, Chief Superintendent?"

"Call it an inference, Mrs. Brighton."

"We prefer not to air our dirty laundry in public—that was Adrian's mistake. That being said, unlike the Tories, we have always welcomed a diversity of opinion and open debate in the Labour Party. It is true that Adrian represents the more radical left-wing element of the party, while Richard favored a more middle-of-the-road approach, the 'Third Way,' if you like."

"What about you, Mrs. Brighton?"

She regarded him coolly. "What about me?"

"Which approach do you favor?"

"That's my business, Chief Superintendent."

Touché, thought Powell. "Would it be fair to say that there were bad feelings between Turner and your husband?"

"I can't speak for Adrian, but I know that Richard respected his views as a legitimate expression of one element of opinion within the party. He never took political debates personally."

"Debate is one thing, but what about personal attacks? I understand that Turner was quite vocal in accusing your husband of selling out Labour's principles over Dockside."

"Adrian tends to get carried away at times," she said in a flat voice.

The thought occurred to Powell that *that* could well turn out to be the understatement of the year. "What about Charles Mansfield?" he continued. "Correct me if I'm wrong, but I understand that Mansfield shared your husband's views on Dockside."

Her expression hardened. "Mansfield has always supported development for development's sake. In the case of Dockside, he had the gall to accuse Richard of being an opportunist—of stealing from the Conservative program, as if they had one! Although I suppose screwing the most vulnerable members of society might qualify as a platform," she added bitterly.

"I will tell you something, Mrs. Brighton, if you promise to keep it in strict confidence."

"Of course."

"We received an anonymous phone call a couple of days ago accusing Mansfield of having a financial interest in Dockside—of being in a conflict-of-interest position, in effect. I'd be interested in hearing your reaction."

She shook her head in disgust. "I wouldn't put anything past him, but I find it difficult to believe that even he could be that stupid."

"That was my initial reaction as well, but Mansfield seems to be taking the whole thing quite seriously. I think he believes that Adrian Turner made the call for political reasons."

"That's impossible! Adrian would never do anything like that."

"How can you be certain?"

"I—I just know, that's all." There was something in her voice.

"I don't know quite how to put this, Mrs. Brighton, but there was a second call, possibly from a different person. The caller suggested that you and Adrian Turner have been seen together lately."

"Seen together? What's that supposed to mean?"

"The suggestion was, I think, that you and Turner are having an affair."

Her eyes flashed angrily. "It was Mansfield, wasn't it?"

"It's possible."

"That pompous little prig!"

"There isn't actually any hard evidence that he made the call."

"Who else would stoop to using such tactics?" she asked, the question obviously intended to be rhetorical.

"All right, let's assume for the moment that it *was* Mansfield who made the call. Do you have any explanation for why he might do such a thing?"

She appeared to consider this for a moment. "Petty spitefulness," she suggested unconvincingly.

Powell had the impression she was holding something back.

She brushed a strand of hair from her face. "I mean, if Mansfield thought that Adrian had accused him of wrongdoing, he was probably just trying to get back at him."

Powell was still not satisfied. Time to cut to the chase, he thought. His eyes met hers. "*Have* you been seeing Adrian Turner, Mrs. Brighton?"

"That's my business, don't you think?" Her gaze was unwavering. Before Powell could reply, she continued in a measured voice, "If you must know, yes, I've seen quite a lot of Adrian recently. However, the reason has to do with politics, not romance—if that is what you were thinking. A short time after Richard was killed, Adrian contacted me. He wanted to talk about ways of healing the rift that had developed within the party over Dockside. It was too soon—I mean politics was the last thing on my mind, but he persisted. I eventually agreed to see him about a week ago at his office. We've met a couple of times since at my flat."

"I'm a bit puzzled, Mrs. Brighton. Why would Turner want to meet with you to discuss an issue about which he and your late husband disagreed so strongly?"

"For the good of the party. He knows I have some influence and there is an election coming up in two years. If we don't get our act together, the only beneficiaries will be Charles Mansfield and his gang of bandits."

"What was the upshot of these meetings?"

She raised an eyebrow. "If I tell you, will it go beyond here?"

"Not if it has no bearing on the case."

"All right. I agreed to lend my support to Adrian's bid for mayor and to try to bring along as many of Richard's supporters on the council as I can. And, in case you're wondering, Chief Superintendent, I *did* think about what my husband would have wanted."

"And what might that be, Mrs. Brighton?"

"To do whatever it takes to keep the Conservatives from winning."

"I've been told that your husband had political ambitions beyond Southwark Council . . ."

She stared at her hands, which were folded in her lap. "Richard had a certain quality, call it charisma, leadership ability, whatever you like. He was young, quick on his feet, and not unattractive, which seems to be a prerequisite in politics these days. To answer your implied question, Chief Superintendent, I think he could have gone as far as he wanted." She looked up at him.

Now for the tricky bits, he thought. "Just one or two more questions, Mrs. Brighton, and I'll let you get back to your shop. I have to ask you something that may be upsetting, so please don't take it personally."

"I'm a big girl, Chief Superintendent."

"I mentioned before the importance of exploring any

possible association between your husband and Clive Morton. We've learned that Morton was a heavy user of cocaine; is there any possibility that your husband was in any way involved with drugs?"

"Absolutely none," she replied without hesitation. "One or two glasses of wine with dinner was the extent of Richard's dependence on drugs."

Powell nodded. "One last question, Mrs. Brighton: If your husband was confronted by a thief or thieves on the night in question, do you think he would have tried to run away?"

She thought about this for a moment. "It would depend on the circumstances, wouldn't it? I don't know . . . If I had to guess, I'd say he would probably have stood his ground and tried to talk his way out of it." She smiled sadly. "He was a politician, after all."

As Powell walked back to Sloane Square tube station, he reflected on his conversation with Helen Brighton. He was disappointed, having hoped for more, unaware that he now had everything he needed.

CHAPTER 26

Powell spent the next morning dodging Merriman, who had been sending him a steady stream of increasingly belligerent e-mail messages demanding to know how he was getting on with his assignment. He had been tasked by Merriman to contribute to the Assistant Commissioner's blueprint for the future of the Metropolitan Police Service by writing the section on "Administrative Streamlining and Client Service Enhancement in the New Millennium." As he read the latest message, he felt like puking. He tried not to think about the close call he had had earlier that morning when he had nearly been trapped by the AC in the library on the twelfth floor, only managing to elude detection by hiding behind one of the reading desks. Turning off his computer, he decided that it might be prudent under the circumstances to fall back to a more secure position. He left messages for Black and Evans to meet him for lunch at the Fitzrovia and then sneaked out of the building by way of the underground car park.

The sky was a hazy gray dome with a faint hint of sun, so he decided to take his chances and walk. Through Queen Anne's Gate with its early-eighteenth-century houses, mellowed dark brick, black iron railings, and painted doors; across Birdcage Walk into the Horse Guards Road—which separated the green jewel of St. James' Park, sparkling with flowers and its lake filled with exotic ducks—from the austere backside of Whitehall; then across the processional sweep of the Mall into Waterloo Place under the watchful eye of the Duke of York (who it is said was placed on his high granite pillar one hundred and twenty-four feet above the pavement to put him beyond the reach of his creditors). Before proceeding into Lower Regent Street, Powell paused to light a cigarette and to compare notes with Captain Scott, with whom he felt a certain kinship.

Twenty minutes later, he was safely ensconced in the Fitzrovia Tavern chatting with Celia Cross about Jill Burroughs.

"You can't imagine what a load off my mind it was to see 'er face, Mr. Powell," Celia said.

Powell took a blissful sip of beer. "Believe me, I know what you mean. The poor girl feels terrible about the way things turned out."

Celia drew herself up to full height behind the bar. "Well, it wasn't 'er fault, was it? It was that toffee-nosed boyfriend of 'ers. She won't be sorry to see the back of 'im, I reckon."

"Did she say when she was leaving?"

"She was trying to book the first available flight to

Toronto." The publican paused thoughtfully. "I'd 'ave her back in a minute, but I suppose it's the best thing really. She's seen a bit of the world, 'ad a bit of a fling, but there's no place like 'ome I always say."

"I'll drink to that," Powell responded, raising his glass.

He was interrupted by a familiar voice. "You're incorrigible, sir."

He turned to see the smiling face of Sarah Evans, with Black filling the doorway behind her. "We were wondering what happened to you," she remarked.

He sighed heavily. "It's a harrowing tale, Evans. Perhaps I'll tell you about it some day."

"Merriman is looking for you, by the way."

"Really? I wonder why he doesn't just send me an e-mail." He turned to Celia. "Would you mind if we used the Writer's Bar? We'd prefer not to be disturbed."

She winked knowingly. "Say no more, Mr. Powell. I'll bring you down some sandwiches."

They ordered their drinks and then made their way downstairs to the dark-paneled room where Powell had interviewed Simon Snavely, the drug-addled Phantom of the Fitzrovia.

When they were settled, Powell turned to Detective-Sergeant Black. "Why don't you start, Bill?"

"Well, sir, a couple of things. First off, I talked to Samantha Jones again—Morton's dinner companion the evening he was killed—to try to narrow down the timing. Apparently, Morton received a phone call at the restaurant sometime between eleven and eleven-thirty. She says she doesn't know who it was. They left together a short time later, and she says she never saw him again."

"That would only be an hour or so before Morton was murdered, perhaps considerably less than that," Powell observed.

"Yes, sir. And Covent Garden isn't that far from Leicester Court."

"It looks like someone called him to arrange a meeting later that night," Evans piped in. "A meeting from which Morton never returned," she added melodramatically.

"It had to be someone he knew."

Evans frowned. "Sir?"

"Who else would call him at eleven o'clock at night when he was on the job, as it were?"

"I've covered the ground between the restaurant and Leicester Court," Black continued. "I've asked everybody I can think of along the way who might have seen him. Nothing, I'm afraid, sir."

Powell grunted.

"There's something else, sir. I took the liberty of having a little chat with Simon Snavely. I bumped into him on my way to his flat. He was busking ouside King's Cross Station, reading some of his—" he grimaced "—er, verse. Based on your description, I knew it was him."

"Did you toss a penny in his hat?"

"I didn't want to encourage him, sir. Anyway, it's been bothering me, sir. Snavely was here on the Saturday evening Morton was giving your friend Jill a hard time. We know he has a yen for her and has a drug problem, which no doubt affects his judgment—maybe he took offense at Morton's carrying-on and confronted him the following Monday night."

"Then bashed him on the head and slit his throat? Rather an extreme reaction, don't you think?"

"Now hatred is by far the longest pleasure; Men love in haste, but they detest at leisure," Black pronounced solemnly.

"Not that I would presume to disagree with Lord Byron," Powell rejoined, "but I think we had better take this a step at a time. What was the gist of your conversation with Snavely?"

"I asked him about his whereabouts on the night in question, but he said he couldn't remember. He seemed a bit edgy and he was obviously high on something. He started babbling on about his rights, so I gave it up."

"He does have a prior for selling cocaine," Powell remarked to no one in particular. "Perhaps Morton was a customer of his."

"Aren't we forgetting something?" Evans blurted out. "Snavely has no known connection with Richard Brighton."

Powell looked at her. "You raise a good point, Evans."

She shifted uncomfortably in her chair.

"Unless, of course, there *is* no connection between the two murders," he mused.

This caught Evans's attention. "What about Sir Reggie . . . ?"

"There is no way he can be absolutely certain that the same weapon was used in both attacks. He's offered us an opinion that must be weighed together with all of the other evidence. We have to at least consider the possibility that he's wrong."

The seconds stretched out tautly as they all considered the implications of this scenario. If the two murders were in fact committed by different villains, the situation could well be hopeless, particularly if the crimes fell into the random violence category, as suspected initially in Brighton's case. "I don't know about you two," Powell said eventually, "but my brain is starting to hurt." He drained his pint and then lit a cigarette, exhaling a vast cloud of smoke into the air above his colleagues. Evans looked annoyed. "What about you, Evans? You were going to tell me something yesterday in the Back Hall."

"Er, yes, sir. I had another visit with Tess Morgan." Evans described the community activist's reaction to the mention of Clive Morton's name and her subsequent visit to Tess's daughter's school. "I rang Ms. Morgan first thing this morning to confirm the headmistress's statement." She paused, looking very serious.

"Yes, Evans?"

"She admitted that her daughter, Rachel, had a drug problem. She used to hang out with her mates in Soho, and on one occasion she ended up at a party at Clive Morton's flat. Ms. Morgan wouldn't go into details, but I gather it was a pretty horrendous experience for the girl. Tess wanted to bring a complaint against him, but Rachel wouldn't cooperate. She didn't want to get her friends in trouble, apparently."

"So there is at least one person we can connect with

both Richard Brighton and Clive Morton," Powell observed carefully. "And she had good reason to hate them both."

Evans nodded bleakly.

CHAPTER 27

Powell started off by summarizing the results of his various interviews with Charles Mansfield and Adrian Turner. "Mansfield seems convinced that it was Turner who placed that first call accusing him of having his finger in the Dockside pie. The intent, one presumes, was to damage him politically. However, it doesn't stand up when you look at it. Why tip the police off to something that may or may not involve an actual crime, when you could take it to a rival politician, or directly to the council, for maximum political impact? Whether the story turned out to be true or not wouldn't really matter at the end of the day—the seeds of doubt would have been planted. In fact, reporting an unsubstantiated allegation to us is probably the best way to ensure that the story *doesn't* get out; after all, we're hardly going to blab it to the press. Strangely enough, this does not seem to have occurred to Mansfield."

"Mansfield must have made the second call, then,

about Turner and Mrs. Brighton," Black ventured. "As a way to get back at Turner."

"That's my guess. But based on my reading of Helen Brighton, I don't think it's true."

"What *about* Turner?" Evans asked. "He's benefited as much as Mansfield from Brighton's death, hasn't he?"

Powell frowned. "I'm not sure what to make of young Adrian. Apart from stirring things up in the borough and working to save the rain forests in British Columbia—"

"What did you say?" Evans interjected.

Powell described the environmental posters in Turner's office.

"Tess Morgan had an anti-logging poster in her flat," she said slowly.

Powell shrugged. "It's not an unpopular cause, unless . . ."

"Unless what?"

Powell looked at her. "Perhaps Mansfield got it wrong—I mean, right idea, wrong person. What if Adrian Turner is having an affair with Tess Morgan, not Helen Brighton?"

"I don't understand—"

"Look, if Turner *was* putting the make on Helen Brighton, it might be viewed as Machiavellian—an attempt to unite the party behind him by uniting, as it were, with his late rival's wife. However, it would be wholly unethical, to say the least, if he were involved with Tess Morgan. Here is a man who has been elected to act objectively, in the best interests of his constituents, voting on a project whose chief opponent is the woman he's sleeping with. If it ever got out . . ."

"We don't know that he *is* sleeping with her," Evans pointed out.

"You're right, but you have to admit it's an intriguing scenario. Let's say Brighton found out about it and threatened to go public . . ."

"But how does Morton fit into it?" Black asked.

Powell sighed. "We keep coming back to that, don't we?" He stared into his empty glass. "It all boils down to motive: Who benefits? I suspect that opportunity won't be much of a problem."

"Still, it probably wouldn't hurt to determine who-was-where-when at the times in question, sir," Black suggested, always the steady tortoise.

Powell nodded. "We should have done that a long time ago, Bill. While you're at it, pull Snavely in and wring him dry. There is something about that lad that sets my teeth on edge. And Evans, you'd better get on with Tess Morgan's tenants committee. I still don't think we can rule out the possibility that there may be some-one lurking in the shadows."

"Yes, sir. I've got the list of the names from Tess Morgan. I'll get started this afternoon."

Powell was suddenly seized with an overwhelming sense of certainty that he was overlooking something important, or rather looking at it the wrong way round. He frowned. His train of thought was interrupted by the arrival of Celia Cross, laden with a plate of ham-and-cheese sandwiches and a tray of drinks.

The weather took a turn for the worse that evening as Powell lounged about in Tony Osborne's flat in

Soho listening to scratchy gems from his host's record collection and drinking his Scotch. Cream, the Yardbirds, John Mayall and the Bluesbreakers, and a glass of the Macallan. Life could be worse, he thought, listening to the rain rattle against the windowpane. He just wished he could get his mind off the case and relax. He pulled back the curtain and peered out. A yellow streetlamp smeared against a dark, wet sky and a car swishing by. He couldn't explain it, but he had a sudden urge to call Marion. He checked his watch and did a quick calculation. It would be nearly noon in Vancouver; he might be able to catch her in before she left for lunch. He reached for his wallet and extracted the crumpled piece of paper on which he had written the numbers for her office at the University of British Columbia and her apartment. He picked up his mobile phone from the coffee table. He pressed the numbers and waited several seconds for the overseas connection. He got up from the sofa and turned down the stereo.

A familiar voice at the other end: "Marion Powell."

"Why aren't you out stalking totem poles?"

"Erskine?"

"How soon they forget. How are you, love?"

"I'm fine. I've been waiting for you to call. I was beginning to wonder if you'd come down with a case of Soho-itis."

"I've been tied up at work. It's a dog's life in the Met."

"How's the case coming?"

"Things are starting to get interesting. It feels a bit like the lull before the proverbial storm."

"Erskine, is everything all right?" There was a note of concern in her voice.

"Why do you ask?"

"I don't know. You sound . . . detached."

"As oppose to engaged?"

"You know what I mean. It's not like you to call in the middle of the day."

"I miss you."

"Me, too." Over muffled voices in the background, she said, "Erskine, I've got to run off to a meeting. Why don't you ring me later?"

"I'll ring you tomorrow night. At your apartment, around ten your time?"

"All right."

"Until then."

"Erskine?"

"Yes."

"Have you given any more thought to coming over this summer? It looks like I'll be finished with my research project by the middle of August. You'd get a chance to see Peter and David, and we could do the tourist thing together for a few weeks . . ."

"We'll see. How are the boys?"

"They're fine. Look, I have to go. I'll talk to you tomorrow."

"Right."

After he rang off, he continued to pace back and forth. He could hear the faint wailing of a police siren. He walked over to the sideboard and poured himself another drink. On his way back to the sofa, he cranked up Long John Baldry. Just as he was starting to feel sorry for himself, his telephone began to warble insistently. He got up once again and turned down the volume. "Powell," he said irritably.

"It's Paul Atherton. Sorry to bother you . . ."

"What's up?" He was suddenly alert.

"It's probably nothing, some sort of hoax, I expect, but I've received a letter—" a slight hesitation "—I suppose you could call it a threat."

"When?"

"Earlier this evening at the office. I'm working late tonight," he explained. "I heard a banging on the door. By the time I got there, whoever it was had gone, but there was an envelope under the door with my name on it. There was a note inside. I have it here." A crinkling of paper. " 'If you don't pack it in you'll end up like Brighton,' " he read in monotone voice.

"That's it?"

"I'm afraid so."

"Is it handwritten or typed?"

"Looks like your standard computer printing."

"Where are you now?"

"I'm still at the office."

"Where do you plan to spend the night?"

"I've been staying with my girlfriend in Marylebone as you suggested."

"How long are you going to be at the office?"

"Another couple of hours, I should think."

Powell consulted his watch. Eight-thirty. "I'd like to see you for a few minutes. Would you mind if I stopped by in, say, forty minutes?"

"I'm not going anywhere, Chief Superintendent."

"Right. See you then."

After he'd rung off, Powell sat staring out the window for a considerable length of time.

CHAPTER 28

The rain had stopped, but a light mist hung in the air, creating a watery halo around the streetlamp. He thought about calling a cab but decided on the tube. He hoped that the short walk to Piccadilly Circus station would help clear his head. As he was heading out the door, umbrella in hand, his mobile phone began to ring once again. He fumbled for it in his jacket pocket. "Yes," he snapped.

"It's Jill. Did I catch you at a bad time?"

"No—no, of course not. I was just heading out, that's all."

"Then I did catch you at a bad time."

"I've always got time for you. How's it going?"

"All right, I guess. I'm catching a flight home tomorrow afternoon. I'll have to pack tomorrow morning, so I—I was hoping that we might get together tonight for a coffee, for old times' sake."

"I'd like that. Where are you now?"

"My hotel in Paddington."

He thought quickly. By the time he finished with Atherton and got back to the West End, it could be quite late. "Look, I've got to meet someone in Southwark," he said. "Do you know where Shad Thames is?"

"Just east of Tower Bridge, right?"

"That's it. Do you know how to get there by tube?"

"I'm sure I can figure it out."

"You take the Bakerloo Line from Paddington Station to Elephant and Castle, then switch to the Northern Line for London Bridge. You go along Tooley Street, turn left into Weaver's Lane, then under Tower Bridge. It's about a ten-minute walk, or you could take a cab. Have you got that?"

Jill laughed. "Clear as mud."

"The chap's name is Paul Atherton. His office is a few doors past the Pizza Express. Why don't you meet me there in about an hour? If there's no sign of life, just knock. When I'm finished, we can decide what to do. All right?"

"Sounds good. See you in a bit."

"Cheers."

He stepped outside and locked the door behind him.

In Great Windmill Street, a knot of people had gathered outside a bar around a figure sprawled on the pavement. Powell identified himself as a policeman and made his way to the front. The man, who looked to be in his early twenties with matted blond hair, was semiconscious, muttering incoherently. Powell squatted down to have a closer look. He was wearing a tattered T-shirt, soaked with vomit, and a cursory examination of the needle tracks on his tattooed arms told the story. Powell lifted the man's wrist. His skin felt clammy, the pulse slow and weak. It was hard to tell in the lurid neon light, but the man's face appeared to have a slightly bluish cast. Powell guessed he had overdosed and was slipping into a coma. He got to his feet and put in a 999 call on his mobile phone.

A few minutes later, sirens were wailing up Shaftsbury Avenue, then a police car squealed around the corner, followed a few seconds later by an ambulance. Powell chatted with the two constables, one of whom he remembered from a training course at which he had lectured, while the paramedics attended to the victim. It was nearly half an hour before he was able to get away, and as he hurried to the tube station, he rang Paul Atherton to let him know he'd be there shortly.

The twin turrets of Tower Bridge soared above him, massive steel skeletons, clad with stone, strong enough to support the thousand-ton bascules that lifted to allow ships to pass up the Thames. The elevated walkway joining the two towers and the heavy arc of the suspension cables shone in the mist with an unearthly blue light, casting an eerie, slightly sinister pallor on the stonework. It reminded him of the junky's face. Must be a trick of the atmosphere, he told himself as he entered Shad Thames. The narrow street, which felt claustrophobic with its dripping brick walls and shadowy walkways, was deserted. If it wasn't for the faint glow of the Pizza Express sign, it might have been fifty years ago.

Paul Atherton opened the door as soon as he knocked.

Powell apologized for being late.

"Not to worry, Chief Superintendent. I'll be here for a while yet."

"No rest for the wicked, eh?"

Atherton smiled. "You might say that. Let's go into my office."

Powell followed him to the back of the building.

They sat as before: Atherton behind his desk and Powell in the chair opposite. There was a green shaded lamp on the desk, otherwise the room was unlit. Something about the room seemed different to Powell but he couldn't put his finger on it.

"Where's the note?" Powell asked.

Atherton reached across the desk and handed him an envelope. He examined it carefully. A standard white business-size envelope with a single word printed on it: ATHERTON. He opened it and carefully extracted the paper inside. He unfolded it and read the words aloud. " 'If you don't pack it in you'll end up like Brighton.' What do you make of it?"

Atherton shrugged. "I'm not sure what to make of it. I'm not used to receiving death threats, Chief Superintendent."

"You think it's a threat, then?"

Atherton looked slightly irritated. "What else could it be?"

"One could interpret it in a more positive light, a warning perhaps from someone concerned about your welfare."

Atherton frowned. "I hadn't thought of that. I suppose our last conversation had me imagining the worst. That *is* what you advised, isn't it?"

"It's always better to be safe than sorry, Mr. Atherton."

"Do you think it can be traced?"

"I doubt it. Computer printers are fairly anonymous. The point is, it does seem to fit the pattern, if one assumes that there is someone out there willing to go any lengths to stop Dockside: Brighton and Morton dead and an anonymous phone call that at first glance appears to be politically damaging to Charles Mansfield. The only thing that doesn't fit is the call we received about Adrian Turner and Helen Brighton." Responding to the look of puzzlement on Atherton's face, Powell explained about the second anonymous call.

"That was probably just Mansfield trying to get back, don't you think?"

Powell regarded him with interest. "That's not an unreasonable assumption, assuming, of course, that it was Turner who made the first call."

"You're right. It's not as if Turner is the only one who is against me."

An interesting way of putting it, Powell thought. "You are referring, I take it, to Tess Morgan," he said.

"Who else?" Atherton responded bitterly.

"The call was made by a man," Powell pointed out.

"It could have been one of the other members of her band of antis."

"Perhaps, but the thing that's been bothering me—" Powell's response was cut short by a loud crashing sound upstairs, followed by a series of muffled thumps.

He glanced at the ceiling, then at Atherton, who regarded him stone-faced. His eyes were drawn to the small glass cabinet on the wall behind the developer. He now realized what was different about the room. There was only one dueling pistol in the baize-lined case.

He looked back at Atherton and found himself staring down the barrel of the missing pistol.

CHAPTER 29

Atherton smiled. "Oh, it's real, all right. A forty-eight bore percussion dueling pistol and highly effective at short range. It was made by Rigby of London in eighteen-twenty. Unfortunately, its mate has a broken hammer, but this little beauty is quite functional, I can assure you. A tribute to the gunmaker's art, don't you think? And, in case you have any ideas, the hammer is fully cocked and I am an excellent shot."

"What's this all about?" Powell asked, his gut churning, realizing too late what had been simmering away in his subconscious for some time.

"Please, Chief Superintendent, take some credit. I think you know exactly what it's all about. Why don't you—"

There was another loud commotion upstairs. It sounded like stamping feet. Atherton shook his head sadly. "Apparently Ms. Burroughs finds my hospitality lacking."

Powell had forgotten all about Jill. Without thinking, he started to get to his feet, his heart pounding. Atherton followed him with the pistol, keeping it pointed at his chest.

"Please sit down, Chief Superintendent. There is absolutely nothing you can do for her."

Powell sat down slowly, keeping his eyes locked on Atherton's.

"It's unfortunate, really," Atherton continued, "for both of you. If your young lady friend hadn't nearly run over me outside the Fitzrovia that night—well, who knows how it might have turned out? As it was, I recognized her when she came here tonight to meet you. I put two and two together and, well, here we are."

Powell's mind raced. He tried to think. What had Celia Cross said about the night that Simon Snavely had tried to follow Jill home? There was a man outside the pub with something wrong with his leg, and Jill had nearly bowled him over in her haste to reach safety. Realization struck him like a thunderbolt. There was only one more piece of the puzzle—it was worth a shot in the dark. "You had a limp," Powell said.

Atherton smiled. "Very good, Chief Superintendent! I'm impressed. I had to have an excuse, didn't I?" He reached under the desk with his left hand, not taking his eyes or the pistol off Powell. "One doesn't carry one of these around without a good reason. He produced an ornate cane, with a heavy iron head adorned with brass and a polished wood shaft, and placed in on the desk in front of him. Powell stared at the curved metal handle. It was hexagonal in cross section.

"A sword cane is a rather ingenious and practical weapon, when you think of it. This one was made in

India in eighteen-forty and is quite collectible. I could remove the shaft and show you the blade, but that would be a bit awkward under the circumstances. You'll just have to take my word that it is sharp enough to shave with." He paused thoughtfully. "Like I said before, I am truly sorry that it had to turn out this way. I was deeply touched by your obvious concern for my welfare, but that's water under the bridge now." He glanced at his watch. "Now then, I don't have all night. Why don't you explain everything to me so I can be sure you have it right. Don't worry, I'll help you through the tricky bits. I wouldn't want you to shuffle off your mortal coil without becoming fully enlightened, as it were."

"To put *your* mind at ease, you mean. You want to make sure that you're justified in committing another murder."

"*Two* murders, Chief Superintendent. Don't forget about Ms. Burroughs." His voice was chillingly devoid of emotion.

Powell knew that his only hope was to play for time— he refused to look beyond this immediate objective, to think about what might lay in store for both him and Jill. He took a deep breath. "For the longest time, I was distracted by the notion that Richard Brighton and Clive Morton were both killed by someone who was committed to stopping Dockside at any cost. I couldn't have been more wrong, could I? The murders were committed not to stop Dockside, but rather to ensure that it went ahead."

He paused to gauge Atherton's reaction and to gain a few precious seconds. The developer said nothing.

"There are three facts that didn't seem significant when viewed in isolation, but when taken together present a compelling case. First off, you are one of the few people involved who had connections with both Brighton and Morton. Brighton was ostensibly your chief political booster, and Morton was an investor. Secondly, the anonymous call to us about Charles Mansfield's alleged interest in Dockside didn't make any sense—it was as if it were intended to have zero political impact. The real objective was to divert attention away from the person who made the call. And, finally, I get the impression that prior to Brighton's death, the tide had begun to turn against Dockside. Mrs. Brighton tells me that her husband was beginning to have second thoughts—"

"That bastard!" Atherton exploded. "He was only concerned about a handful of rabble-rousers and saving his own political skin—he didn't give a damn about me." There was a feverish intensity in his voice. "Brighton came to the office that night, said he was thinking of having Dockside sent back to the planning committee for further study. That would have taken months, time I didn't have. I suggested we go for a walk to talk it over." He smiled crookedly. "He said he owed me that much." He stroked the sword cane's shaft. "On a whim, I took this along. I told him I'd turned my ankle playing squash. I led him down along the quay. It was foggy that night, and there was no one else around. I pleaded with him, told him I would lose everything if there was any more delay, but he wouldn't listen, said a project should proceed on its own merit after thorough study. I was desperate. I lost my shirt in the 'ninety property market crash, and there was no way I was going to let my last chance to get back on my feet slip away. I offered him a share of the profit, ten percent, if he could push Dockside through the council. He got up on his high horse and threatened to expose me, said he wanted nothing more to do with a sleazy operator like me." Atherton's face contorted into a mask of pure malice. "He called me pathetic and turned his back on me." He gripped the head of the stick. "I let the son of a bitch have it." His face suddenly went slack. "The rest was easy. I pushed him over the railing into the river, and that was that. At first, I was worried about what I'd done, but when support for Dockside surged out of respect for the wishes of the late beloved councillor, I knew it was brilliant."

"What about Morton?" Powell asked.

"Ah, yes. Poor departed Clive. We were introduced last year by a mutual acquaintance at my club. We got talking; I told him about Dockside, and he mentioned that he always wanted to open his own restaurant. I needed funds at the time to renew my option on the warehouse property. He was willing to put up the money in exchange for the restaurant and ten percent of the ultimate profit." He frowned. "Unfortunately, Clive insisted on a clause in the contract that obliged me to refund his investment at any time upon request. I was so desperate, I was willing to sign anything. About three weeks ago, Clive came to me and demanded his money back, said he'd run up some drug debts."

The developed sneered. "He was nothing but a frigging junky, scum of the bloody earth. Anyway, I told him I wasn't able to come up with the funds, and he threatened to sue me. I couldn't afford to fight him in court, and even if I'd won, the adverse publicity would have killed the project. So I had to stop him. I arranged to meet him that Saturday night at the Fitzrovia Tavern, the night your friend upstairs bumped into me outside the pub. I told him I had a proposition to make. We were to meet at the pub at ten o'clock. My intention was to wait outside until closing time. I thought he might head into Soho to indulge in one of his vices. I planned to follow him and wait for an opportunity to corner him in some dark alley. I hadn't really thought it through. I don't mind admitting I was nervous. After all, it wasn't like the first time—with Clive it was, well, premeditated. Anyway, it all turned for naught. There must have been some sort of kerfuffle in the pub, because just before eleven-thirty the police arrived. Needless to say, I got the hell out of there."

It occurred to Powell, out of the blue, that if it hadn't been for Simon Snavely, Clive Morton might well have enjoyed two fewer days on this earth. He assessed Atherton's demeanor, trying to appear casual. The developer's face was expressionless, the pistol still leveled at Powell's chest. There was another thump upstairs.

"So, how did you finally pull it off?" Powell prompted.

He spoke mechanically. "I called him on Monday and apologized profusely for standing him up. I told him my girlfriend had taken ill. We arranged to meet that evening. He told me to ring him at a restaurant in Covent Garden around eleven o'clock. We met in Leicester Square at eleven-thirty. I suggested we repair to my club where we could talk. I led him into a little alley that could be construed as a shortcut to Shaftsbury Avenue and let him go ahead. Then I—what's that Beatle's song, 'Maxwell's Silver Hammer'?" He frowned thoughtfully. "He was only unconscious, of course, so I had to finish the job. He bled more than I expected, but I don't suppose he felt much." He spoke with an air of clinical detachment.

Powell swallowed. "And the apple?"

"That was a rather cunning diversion, don't you think? How many restaurateurs must there be in London who would love to draw and quarter poor old Clive and serve him up on a platter?"

Powell had to suppress a wave of panic. He was attempting to carry on an extended conversation with a raving bloody psychopath, and he was running out of things to say. He quickly considered his chances, bleak as they were. It was true that Atherton only had one shot, although he could hardly miss at this range. He thought about going out in a blaze of glory with a desperate lunge across the desk, but there was Jill to think about. He decided he had no option except to try to play for more time. "You obviously had it all thought out, Paul," he said slowly, "but surely it must have occurred to you that I wouldn't have come here alone tonight."

Atherton smiled. "Nice try, Chief Superintendent. Oh, I think you had your suspicions, all right, but my guess is you were waiting to see if Ms. Burroughs could identify me before you made up your mind. I suppose you'll be telling me next that the place is surrounded by cops."

Powell looked at him placidly. "It is, actually."

A flicker of doubt crossed Atherton's face. Before he

could reply, the silence was pierced by the sharp, warbling sound of a telephone. Powell hardly dared to breathe. He looked down at his pocket, then back at Atherton. "You see, Paul? They're checking up on me."

Atherton's eyes narrowed suspiciously. "Let it ring," he said.

"If I don't answer it, they'll force their way in. It's the drill in situations like this. Put down the gun, Paul, and we can sort this thing out."

"Give it to me," Atherton hissed. "And don't make any sudden movements."

Powell reached into his jacket pocket and extracted his mobile phone. It continued to chirp insistently. The sound seemed unnaturally loud amidst the taut silence.

"Now place it on the desk very carefully and push it over. Slowly," Atherton cautioned.

Powell started to comply. Then, with a bloodcurdling yell, he flicked the phone into the developer's face as if it were a red-hot coal and hit the floor.

CHAPTER 30

The pistol report was deafening. Powell leapt to his feet and dove across the desk at the developer. Atherton's chair toppled over backward, sending both men crashing to the floor. Powell pinned Atherton with his right forearm across his throat, while trying to get him to drop the pistol by repeatingly smashing his right hand against the leg of the overturned chair. Eventually, the pistol clattered to the floor. Atherton seemed paralyzed; his body was rigid, but he didn't seem to be resisting. His face was expressionless, his eyes staring. Powell could see his mobile phone on the floor against the wall a few feet in front of them. He knew the next part would be the tricky bit. "All right, Paul," he said between ragged breaths. "I'm going to get off you now. I'd like you to stay there on the floor until I tell you to get up. The other policemen will be here in a few seconds," he lied. If he could get his hands on the sword cane, he could make the call and hold Atherton at bay until reinforcements did arrive.

He began to push himself up slowly. He realized too late, as Atherton swung his left arm up, where the sword cane was. The heavy iron head struck him on the side of the head, causing him to cry out. He was conscious of Atherton lowering his arm to strike again. He jammed his elbow into Atherton's face, then scrambled to his feet. He staggered backward against the desk. Atherton was clutching his nose with one hand and moaning, blood streaming between his fingers. He was struggling to push himself up with the other arm.

Powell's head was spinning crazily. Without really thinking about what he was doing, he bent over to pick up the pistol, then lurched toward the door to the right of the desk. It seemed like minutes before he finally got there. He tried the knob, and the door swung open to reveal a dimly lit hall and a flight of ascending stairs. He shut the door behind him and pushed the button to lock it. He leaned back against it for a few seconds, trying to catch his breath, then started up the stairs, supporting himself on the banister, willing himself to move one foot after the other, counting slowly with each step. He tried to imagine that he was nearing the summit of some blizzard-torn Himalayan peak. To stop now was unthinkable—except he was burning up not freezing— one two one two. There was an open archway at the top of the stairs revealing another hallway with closed doors on either side and one at the end.

He tried the door on the left; it was unlocked. It was a bedroom, neatly made up as if it hadn't been used recently.

There was a sudden scrabbling sound behind him. He

whirled around, nearly fainting in the process as his head refused to stop when the rest of him did. When the door across the hall had returned to a vertical position, he reached for the knob.

In the middle of the floor, a wooden chair lay on its side. In the chair, her hands and feet bound with electrical cord and her mouth covered with duct tape, was Jill Burroughs. Her eyes were wide, and by the muffled sounds she was making in her throat, it was evident that she had much to tell him. He locked the door behind him and quickly scanned the room. It appeared to be Atherton's study. There was a bookshelf and a small writing table with a telephone on either side of French windows. Ignoring Jill for the moment, he went over to the table and picked up the phone. It was dead. He cursed silently. He followed the cord under the table and saw that the jack had been pulled from the wall receptacle. He reached under and plugged it in. He placed the receiver to his ear and heard the reassuring tone. He knew that it would be hopeless to call the local police station where he would probably have to wait ages to get through, so for the second time that evening, he rang 999.

When he had finished the call, he rushed over to Jill. He knelt down beside her, put down the pistol, and ripped the tape from her face.

"Ouch!" she said.

"Are you all right?" he asked anxiously.

She nodded vigorously, her eyes frightened. "Is he . . . ?"

He smiled reassuringly. "Don't worry. He knows the game's over. I expect he's a mile away by now. In a few minutes, the place will be swarming with police." He stood up. "Here," he said, bending over to grasp the back of the chair with both hands, "let's get you the right way up so I can untie you." He manhandled the chair into an upright position, then, breathing heavily, leaned on it for a few seconds to support himself. Jill looked at him, concern in her eyes. "Are *you* all right?"

He nodded. "Just a knock on the head, that's all. I'll be fine. Let's get your hands untied." He was working away at the knots, trying to will his head to stop pounding, when he felt Jill stiffen.

"What's that?" she whispered.

He froze. He could hear the faint, unmistakable click of a key turning in a lock. Before he could react, the door burst open and there stood Atherton, eyes wild and white shirt stained with blood, brandishing a gleaming sword.

Powell had no time to think things through. He just knew that he had to draw Atherton away from Jill. He lunged for the French windows, taking it on faith that they must lead somewhere and trying not to think about the drop to the pavement below. Fortunately, the windows were unlocked. As he burst through, he found himself on one of the iron walkways that spanned Shad Thames. He could hear Atherton close behind him, and he could only hope that there was a way out at the other end.

He was about halfway across when he felt a sudden searing pain in his right thigh. He crumpled to his knees, nearly fainting as the sword was wrenched from Atherton's grasp. Eyes streaming with tears, he reached around and pulled out the blade, cutting his hand in the process. It clattered to the iron grating as his pursuer was upon him.

He had no idea where he found the strength, but with a last frantic effort, he managed to roll over on top, grasping Atherton's hair with his injured hand, fingers slippery with blood. He pulled Atherton's head up, then smashed it down on the grating. He wasn't able to apply much force, so, with ghastly determination, he had to do it again and again. He didn't stop until Atherton's body went limp beneath him.

He felt for the handle of the sword and pushed it over the edge. A second later, it landed with a metallic clanging on the cobbles below. He struggled to get to his knees, gasping for breath, and called out to Jill in a hoarse voice to let her know that he was all right. Then, grasping the low railing with both hands, he pulled himself to his feet, grunting with the pain. Supporting his weight on the railing, he hobbled slowly back to Atherton's study.

EPILOGUE

Powell's recollection of the next few days in hospital tended to be episodic—that is, he remembered certain moments with vivid clarity, while much of it remained a blur. They said he'd lost a lot of blood, and he supposed they were giving him something for the pain, which might explain his memory lapses. He was, however, constantly aware of the backdrop of antiseptic smells, starched nurses, and prodding doctors.

He remembered Jill's visit the next morning on the way to Heathrow, her pale face anxious, feeling guilty about leaving. He told her that he was the one who was responsible for nearly getting them both killed. If only he'd twigged a little sooner. He could still see her smile. "Well, you got there in the end," she said. She was looking forward to settling down to a quiet life at university in Toronto, and she promised she would write. The next minute she was gone . . . or perhaps he had drifted off. Then Black and Evans bending over him, offering authoritative medical opinions and chiding him for lying about in bed while crime ran rampant. And a potted plant from his colleagues, which he would undoubtedly manage to kill, and a treacly get well card.

He couldn't remember which day it was that he awoke to find Marion sitting beside his bed, holding his hand. At first he thought he must be dreaming. "I came as quickly as I could." He smiled and squeezed her hand. "You're getting too old for this," she said. Didn't I tell you it's a dog's life? At some point, he became aware that it was Marion who had tried to reach him at Atherton's that night just because she wanted to talk. Thanks, old girl, I'll tell you about it someday. He looked into her eyes, seeing the depth of her concern. "Have you been home yet, love?" She nodded, and he suddenly felt apprehensive.

"I can explain about the garden," he said.

A CONVERSATION WITH GRAHAM THOMAS

Q: Graham, who (or what) was the inspiration for your series hero, Detective-Chief Superintendent Erskine Powell of New Scotland Yard?

A: Powell is undoubtedly an amalgam of various influences and experiences, both literary and personal. It became apparent when I started writing *Malice in the Highlands*, the first book in the series, that he already existed somewhere in my creative unconscious. The experience is rather like writing about someone I know intimately, as opposed to consciously constructing a fictional character.

Q: Let's talk briefly about your pre-Powell life. Would you give us a thumbnail biography of yourself?

A: From the moment I picked up a copy of J. P. Donleavy's *The Ginger Man* as an impressionable youth, I knew I wanted to be a writer. I majored in English literature at university, then switched to biology when I realized that I might have to get a job someday. For the past twenty-five years, I've worked as a professional biologist in the field of fisheries management.

Q: When you introduced Erskine Powell in Malice in the Highlands, *did you envision a series? Or was* Highlands *originally a stand-alone novel?*

A: I always envisioned a series. There are the practical considerations, of course, but from a creative point of view, much of the enjoyment I derive from writing mysteries is the opportunity to continually develop and reveal my hero's character, to test him in new situations. You can't do this in a one-off novel. Also, I think most mystery readers appreciate continuity. It's like cheering on the home team—although every game is different, the star player never lets you down.

Q: Clearly you are not (and never have been, have you?) a Scotland Yard detective; but that aside, how much of Erskine Powell is based on your own experience? Or to ask another way: In what ways is your protagonist similar to—and completely unlike—his creator?

A: Short of signing up for a course of psychoanalysis, I'm not sure how I should answer that! Powell is better-educated, better-looking, and more intuitive than I am. However, like his creator, he is, beneath a somewhat cynical veneer, a romantic at heart. More revealing, perhaps, is the fact that we're both addicted to curry.

Q: What about background research—how vital is that for you?

A: Getting the details right is very important to me. Put it down to my scientific training. Having said that, I am willing to sacrifice verisimilitude, where necessary, to further the story. An example: In my books, Powell is a member of the Yard's Murder Squad, an organization which no longer exists. At one time, senior Scotland Yard detectives were called in by local police forces to investigate difficult or high-profile murder cases, but this is no longer the case. It is, nonetheless, a useful fictional device which enables me to set my stories in a variety of interesting and atmospheric locales such as the Scottish Highlands, the north coast of Cornwall, and the North York Moors. I typically spend more time doing background research for a book and thinking about the story in a fairly unstructured way than actually writing.

Q: Your novels unfold in actual locales, although you sometimes invent town names. What advantages and disadvantages have you discovered with this approach?

A: A vivid sense of place and setting is (I hope) a key element of my novels. In order to strike a balance between realism and literary license, I generally set my stories in a fictional village, which I locate—using plausible, but not overly precise, geographic reference points—near a real town. For example, *Malice in Cornwall* features the imaginary village of Penrick near St. Ives. Similarly, *Malice on the Moors* is set in and around the fictional hamlet of Brackendale, near the town of Kirkbymoorside in North Yorkshire. This approach enables me to realistically describe an actual locale yet allows me to take liberties for plot purposes. And I don't have to worry about somebody who was born and raised in my village taking me to task for getting some detail wrong. The disadvantage? The risk of not pulling if off.

Q: You chose a pseudonym for your novels. What was the thinking behind that?

A: Being a writer with a day job, I basically have a split

personality. A pseudonym seemed the logical expression of this. And it has the added advantage of insulating one from excessive public adulation or derision. (I like to hedge my bets!)

Q: What's the game plan for you—and Erskine Powell —after **Malice in London?**
A: Erskine and I have a number of ideas, including a story set in America. But the truth is, he and I never know where the next murder most foul will take us.